Hallowed Ground

Trevor Wilkinson

ISBN: 978-1-911311-48-5

For
Tristram and Rory.

Prologue

It was a bleak, featureless day, typical of the North Sea in
late February. The ferry passed between the outer moles of
the harbour, ending its six-hour passage from Harwich to the
low-lying coast of Holland. It had been a breezy crossing. A
fresh northerly was sending a short swell down the elongated
concrete neck that led to the ferry terminal, making the task of
berthing alongside more challenging than usual. The Pride of
the Netherlands eventually came to rest, crunching a bit heavily
against the jetty. Not too bad in such awkward weather, thought
Captain Drummond. Even though Henry Drummond had been a
ferry captain for longer than he cared to remember, he still took
pride in the way his ship was handled. Having asked the deck
officer to tell the engine room that they had finished with the main
engines, he was now free to turn his hand to the irksome round
of formalities that were a routine part of the job. Like most of his
breed, he much preferred the feel of a ship on the open sea to the
officialdom and paperwork that dogged most aspects of life in
harbour.

Recovering from the hypnotic effects of the crossing, groups
of passengers in the main lounge were starting to collect their
belongings. Held together in clusters by some unseen bond, they
surged uncertainly this way and that like flotsam on a beach,
eventually heading in the direction of the exits leading to the car
decks below. The seating area, camouflaged by a thin sprinkling
of plastic packaging and paper cups, would soon be declared a war
zone by the ferry staff and the cleaners would move in. The first
passengers were cautiously finding their way down the narrow
metal companion ladders to the tightly packed cars four decks
below, trying to recall where they had parked nearly seven hours
earlier.

1

At the head of the queue of cars planning a quick exit, a dark blue Renault 605 was attracting attention. For slumped over the steering wheel was the figure of a man, his head and shoulders turned awkwardly to one side, possibly because of the way the ferry had bumped against the jetty. Documents from an open briefcase, including what looked like a passport, were scattered on the front passenger seat suggesting the result of a hurried search. These papers would later reveal the identity of the man in the dirty blue Renault to be an Englishman – perhaps more accurately a man with an English name, as he had the features and sallow skin of a man from the Mediterranean, very likely the Levant.

It mattered little. For whatever his name or the country of his origin, he was dead. And as the Duty Officer of the Dutch Port Authority said to Captain Drummond, dead men don't need passports.

'Dey must haf de ruite papurs,' he growled

Each word was accompanied by gently striking the desk in front of him with an out-stretched hand, his guttural intonation adding emphasis to the seriousness of his observation. Even for a Dutch harbour official he wasn't entirely without humour, as he added with something approaching a twinkle,

'Cadavers may not be fussy, but the Dutch Harbour Authorities are.'

He pushed his chair back and nodded as if to indicate that the subject was closed until the right papers were produced. Captain Drummond, to avoid the possibility of delay – possibly a prolonged one – had already taken his leave and was heading back to the ship's office to make sure that the correct papers were in hand, that the firm of Funeral Undertakers in the harbour town had been alerted. They would know the form. The Renault would have

II

to be moved from blocking the way off the car deck as no vehicles were able to leave the ship, and this could not even be attempted until the body of the driver had been removed. It would take time, and queues of frustrated passengers, anxious to get going on their journey, were lengthening by the minute. Among these a few tasteless comments were already circulating, one to the effect that the old fellow must have been out of his mind to have eaten in the ship's restaurant at all, doubting whether the poor man's Dover sole could ever have seen the Straits of Dover, well not since there had been crocodiles in the Thames. But such attempts at humour did little to lift the gloom or lessen the frustration.

Only one man remained unperturbed. Sitting by himself on one of the slatted wooden benches in the after viewing area, he was hunched inside an anorak against the toneless grey weather. To add to his anonymity, his head was half buried in some sort of trade magazine. He had no plans to go ashore and, had anyone been watching him during the last half hour, it would have been obvious he had no intention of leaving the ferry. Not until he was safely back in Harwich, where he had left his own car parked in the vast, anonymous parking area beside the Harwich ferry terminal facing the low, grey foreshore of Dovercourt Bay.

1.

In most people's lives there are moments that later turn out to have been something of a watershed.

Ben Benbow would look back on the start of the week as just such a turning point. Early on Monday - he was always early for everything - the phone rang in his office. It was Gill Liscombe, a close friend of his for rather more than three years. She was quite simply the most energetic person he knew. When Ben had first launched his Consultancy – specialising in the arcane but profitable business of infrastructure development – her influence had proved an inspiration. Unlike his own more intellectual approach, her plain dealing, take-no-prisoners attitude was a constant source of strength. It was her confidence, her drive that had given life to the promise of later success.

'Ben, darling' she said in a disconcertingly warm voice 'I may have something that will interest you.'

'You most certainly do,' he replied teasingly 'I'm surprised you hadn't noticed.' Toying with thoughts that were unsuitable for a Monday morning, he enjoyed the intimacy of light-hearted banter. 'But, come on, what is it you have that might be of interest?

'It's a package,' she continued, choosing to ignore the innuendo 'a large one, quite wide and flat like a drinks tray, it's that sort of shape and size.' Ben noticed that the natural warmth of her voice had begun to cool, becoming more edgy as she finished 'Shall I bike it over?'

'Yes, do.' said Ben, intrigued by the thought of what it might be. 'By the way, if you don't actually know what it is, how do you know it will interest me?'

Typical of Ben, she thought, having a tendency to turn a subject

1

on its head and look at it from a different angle. Taking nothing for granted was second nature to him, giving him a keen sense of curiosity.

'Who's it from, Gill?'

'It's from a man who's been doing some research for us – for a series of programmes on Greece we were commissioned to make for the BBC.' she paused for a second, 'He left it at our reception, marked clearly for you, Ben Benbow, which I believe is your name? It was yesterday. Seems he knows you through a project you worked on together last year.'

By now, a note of concern was evident in her voice.

'His name's George, George Abbott.'

Ben couldn't work it out - she was definitely on edge about something. But she was right, he did know someone called Abbott. Not all that well, but about a year ago he and George had worked together on a project that had been the brain-child of the Commercial Attaché at the Greek Embassy in London, Constantine Lupradis. George knew him well, which was hardly a surprise, since he appeared to know practically everybody with any connection to Greece. When Ben had put the phone down, he started to recall what he knew about George Abbott.

One of the priorities of the Greek government in the late 1980's had been to give a long overdue boost to their national economy - an economy heavily dependent on agriculture - through encouraging inward investment by foreign companies. Geographically Greece was favourably placed to provide an almost physical link between the European Union and what was then known as the Comecon countries – the communist states on Europe's eastern flank. The idyllic climate, in contrast to the rest of northern Europe, should make it possible to replicate the

2

conditions that a fine climate had had on the thriving economies of the sunshine states in America. Given the right infrastructure, of course, which was why Ben had been called in. Many government officials seemed to think the comparison was sound. The hard part of the task lay in persuading those with the necessary influence and resources to commit themselves; finding the funds to get the project up and running was the real challenge. Handing over money was not a natural gesture for a Greek Government, as Ben remembered only too well.

This was where George Abbott fitted in. A born net-worker, he knew nearly everybody who had any bearing on Greek affairs, and these qualities were evident when they had both gone on a trip to Athens twelve months earlier to see if the project could be got off the ground. George had arranged for them to meet everyone, from the Prime Minister and Finance Minister to platoons of lesser officials who might possibly prove useful. George's wide circle of former colleagues and acquaintances had prompted Ben to create a discreet acronym – *fog* – for Friend of George, which he tacked onto to the names of George's friends on the growing list of contacts and phone numbers in his note-book.

George was clearly a man whose past was of labyrinthine complexity. It was the only sort of past George's countrymen accepted as natural to their birthright. Little was known about him, though Ben's brother-in-law, who had had quite a bit to do with the Foreign Office over the years, suggested that he might have acquired his English name and identity as a result of doing something useful for the British in Cyprus or elsewhere in the eastern Mediterranean. During the Second World War, when he can only have been a boy, George had even been thought to have had a connection with the SOE. In those now distant times, terrible things were done, even by the very young, for the German occupation of Greece had been ruthless.

The old adage about collaboration or treason, like terrorism or freedom fighting, being opposite sides of the same coin, often

3

lead to grim reprisals as old scores were settled. Bitterness between factions, often deep-rooted, could be traced a long way back through many generations, even to the early years of the nineteenth century and the war of liberation from the Ottoman Turks; or even earlier than that, for the continuity of the Greek idea was centuries old.

When they had first met, Ben noticed that George, a man with a reserved but charming manner, treated his past as a completely closed book. That he always preferred to wear a tweed jacket and grey flannel trousers, perhaps to underscore the fact that he really was called Abbott and was as English as they come, was, to say the least, eye-catching.

Wondering what on earth could have prompted George to send him anything, Ben feared it might prove to be some pointless artefact for squeezing lemons that George had found in upper Macedonia or, even worse, an over generous sample of feta cheese. Time would tell.

2.

It wasn't long before the bike from Gala TV arrived, a package
slung across the back of its rider. All parcels are intriguing and
this one was no exception. Covered in an outer layer of brown
paper with his name and address scrawled across it in large
letters, inside was a protective layer of corrugated cardboard. Ben
struggled first with the outer and then with the inner wrapping to
find that it wasn't a tray at all. It was a painting. An oil painting?
He searched through the wrapping paper hoping to find an
explanation, and found nothing. The only thing he had to go on
was that it was from George. But, hang on, as he handled the
frame he found a note had been stuck on the back of the stretcher.
It was a scribble:

> *Ben – For you in case anything happen me. Good instinct, you*
> *know what to do. Βίαστίκα, G*

The phrase 'anything happens to me' sounded ominous; and did
'*biastika*' mean in haste? No doubt it would all become clear later.
He turned to the painting itself.

On stretched canvas, about 30 inches wide by 24 inches deep,
it was framed in finely carved olive wood. As for the painting
itself, he could hardly believe it. It was just a blaze of colour - a
kaleidoscope of mostly primaries , like a bunch of flowers chosen
by a blind florist, if ever such a poor devil was in the wrong job.

At first glance it appeared to have been painted recently and in
common with many of today's paintings Ben found it difficult
to tell whether it had actually been finished. But if it had, it had
been finished in a hurry, that much was evident. Broad brush
strokes, mainly across the middle section of the canvas, had the
look of work done with a purpose, but it had no shape, nor any
recognisable subject so far as Ben could make out. He also noticed
that the paint had been applied thickly. Wondering if it might be
some sort of abstract, he realised such a thought was grasping at
straws. In fact, so startling and unpleasant was its impact, his first

5

impulse was to stand it on the floor facing the wall. That George had nurtured any pretensions of being a painter was news to him, but the initials, GA, in the lower right hand corner suggested that George Abbott might have had a hand in its making.

Bearing in mind the scribbled message, Ben realised he probably had work to do. What could George be on about?

Picking up the phone, he dialled George's number. It rang and rang. No reply, not even an answering service. He then vaguely recalled George saying something about going on holiday, visiting an old haunt of his in the Peleponnese. He couldn't be sure. Anyway, that wouldn't explain a strange painting arriving out of the blue. Bizarre, he thought, and out of character too. Perhaps Gill would know. He called her, but was told she was in post production, putting the finishing touches to a film in one of Gala's editing suites. He left her a message. Later that afternoon she returned his call and they fixed to meet for a drink at a club called the Limpopo, off Old Compton Street. She seemed very keen to meet.

oooooo

Those who knew her at all well said that Gill reminded them of an avalanche – nearly unstoppable once she'd got going. With an open mind and very few prejudices, she was always able to focus her mental energies on the subject under discussion in such a way as to yield a wonderfully simple solution. She had a rather conspiratorial smile which could win most people over to her way of thinking in a matter of seconds. Dark hair, cut quite short with a half fringe, made her look neat, which tempted some of her friends to say that she might look more approachable if her hair sometimes looked more dishevelled.

From an early age Gill had been fascinated by everything to do with films and as she grew older her interest grew stronger. It was a world of illusion and surprise and she thoroughly enjoyed the nearly magical process of putting a film together. Having started her working life as a production assistant – in those days it was thought to be a job you could easily get if you could type – she had taken on a series of progressively more demanding jobs, soon becoming one of the most sought after producers. A little more than a year ago, she had been snapped up by one of London's top production companies, Gala Vision, based in Soho. Her growing professional confidence and reputation had now reached the point where she was beginning to look towards her next obvious step, an opportunity to direct.

As far as Ben was concerned by far her most striking quality was a formidable appetite for getting things done. Her life, certainly the most satisfying moments of it, tended to thrive around activity.

'What's up?' he asked her gently, sensitive to her apparent nervousness.

'Oh Ben,' she said, in a voice tinged with anxiety 'it's all about George Abbott.' She leant across the table towards him adding under her breath 'he's, well, he's been found dead.'

For a moment Ben seemed incapable of processing what he had heard, for only that morning he had been cursing George for being a rubbish painter.

"You mean – a heart attack or something, something like that?'

When y'ure deed, y'ure deed an old saying of his Scottish mother's flitted through his mind, reminding him of death's unarguable finality.

Then, unbidden, he recalled George's note on the back of the painting, *in case anything happen me*: that telepathic warning had proved real enough, his message was now all too easy to understand. George had known that his life was in danger.

'Maybe. I don't know.' Gill was vague. 'This morning we got a message from Stenna Ferries in Harwich saying that a Mr

7

Abbott had died on the crossing to Holland last Friday, found slumped in his car.'

Gill went on to say that some of the papers in his briefcase had her film company's name on them so the ferry company thought he might be on an assignment for us. With nothing else to go on, and no pointer to any next of kin, Gala TV was the only point of contact they had.' She paused, but there was more.

'I turned up his file and there, on top of the scripts, contract notes and various other bits and pieces, was a note written by George asking us to send round to you the parcel he'd left with our receptionist.'

Sipping the mixture of wine and fizzy mineral water, from what appeared to be an unsteady glass, Gill felt greatly relieved that she had at last been able to tell Ben what had been on her mind for much of the day. And at that precise moment she needed the reassurance, the closeness of Ben more than ever.

If earlier he had been a bit puzzled, his thoughts now started chasing a jumble of rather more sinister shadows. All he had to go on was that George, having a premonition he might be going to die, had left him a painting, and that he, Ben, would know exactly what to do. Well, George could just be right: Ben was certainly able to think things through, even to think the so-called unthinkable, making connections where others failed to see the link. He had that sort of mind.

'By the way, Ben, his funeral is on Thursday. At the Greek Orthodox Church, Notting Hill – I don't know when.' Pulling herself together she was quickly becoming her normal self. 'The person arranging everything' she continued, 'is a PA to the Third Secretary at the Greek Embassy, Sue Karamanlis. Why not give her a ring? You know,' her voice fading as she spoke 'what does rather surprise me is the speed of this whole thing. I mean he appears to have died on Friday, it's only Monday now, yet everything seems sorted.' She paused, lost in thought.

And something else had already crossed her mind, why had there been been no autopsy, no post mortem. No cause of death. Nothing. Wasn't that unusual? It seemed clear to Gill that someone from the embassy must have moved very quickly to get it all sorted – very quickly indeed.

3.

The news of George's death made the sequence of events that
followed look even more strange, and by the following morning
Ben was convinced that looking for a reason like a heart attack
as the cause of death was irrelevant. From the note it was clear
that George knew his life was in danger. Now he was under an
obligation, through an uncalled for sort of legacy to discover why
George had popped his clogs. It was up to him.

He realised1 that he was facing not one, but two serious questions.
First, it looked as though George might have been murdered,
which meant that he needed to find out who might be behind
such a ghastly deed. And second, he was the person to de-cipher
the painting. Easy! Well, it shouldn't be as difficult as all that. At
worst, a burst of investigative searching would keep him out of
the pubs.

So he decided to ring the Greek Embassy. Sue Karamanlis was
helpful. Yes, the funeral service was at noon on Thursday, at St
Sophia in the Moscow Road. No, you certainly didn't have to be a
member of the Greek Orthodox Church to attend.

'Any idea how George had died?' he asked, innocently enough.

'He was found dead at the wheel of his car when the ferry
docked.

'No, I really meant *how* he had died, what was the cause of his
death?' Ben said with rather heavier emphasis. 'I mean, it can't
have been a heart attack, or a stroke, can it? When I last saw
him, he looked in great shape – for his age he looked fine.'

'I know. But no-one here seems to know. He died. As you
say, he seemed in good health.' She was beginning to sound
defensive. 'Ben, just how well did you know him?'

Her manner had changed, becoming more on her guard as she spoke. In an instant she had become more interested in Ben, trying to find out just how much he knew about George.

'Quite well, I suppose. About a year ago we spent a week together in Athens on a project, the brainchild of your Commercial Attaché. Ben was beginning to recall the details of their trip. 'In Athens we spent a lot of time with the Trade Minister - including the new one because there was a re-shuffle while we were there. We also had dinner with the Finance Minister one evening. George knew everyone, didn't he?"

'A few too many.' She paused for a second, regretting that her last, unguarded comment may have gone too far. 'He had connections with officials in the government at all levels, as well as politicians and others in the world of business and finance. And other less salubrious characters.'

'Not like me?' Ben chuckled, 'No, Mrs Karamanlis, I'm not being serious. But you're right, there was more to George than a tweed jacket. When we were in Athens we had a free evening and went to a dump in Piraeus, the name I forget – no I don't – I think it was called the *Kovtipi,* which may mean something to you. Anyway we met up with a whole host of his friends, including a very charming character called Androustes.'

'Leonides Androustes! So you've met him? By the way, Ben, please do call me Sue. Leonides is very special. His opponents say he's a vain, opinionated man, but they can't have known him very well. Of course nearly everyone connected with Greek politics has some sort of a reputation, a few skeletons in his cupboard, and he is no exception. But all I can tell you is that he really does care about everything to do with Greece, the Greek ideal.'

'I seem to remember' Ben went on 'that later that same evening we gate-crashed a wedding party. Somewhere near the waterfront. Anyway, Leonides and I had a grand time dancing up and down the jetty with all kinds of people. You should know, Sue, though not a West Indian, I was born and brought up in Trinidad, so I can dance every bit as well as most Greeks. Perhaps not as well as Androustes, come to think of it.'

'Oh, really!'

Her opinion of Ben was shifting. His easy charm and remarks about dancing seemed to have brought about a change of heart. A man who enjoyed dancing was her kind of man.

'Of course Androustes can dance; most Greek men can. Once upon a time he was known to be something of a patriot, what you might call an Hellene. In those days patriotism helped you in Greek politics. But that was many years ago; in more recent times life hasn't been easy for men like that. Incidentally, he hopes to come to London for George's funeral.' Her manner towards Ben had definitely shifted, using the sort of judgemental innuendos often used between colleagues. 'I look forward to seeing you on Thursday. There's more I can tell you about George.'

She ended the conversation as though someone had come into her office, someone who shouldn't hear that she was talking about George Abbott, let alone what she might have to say about him. She had been abrupt.

4.

Moscow road runs west from Queensway towards Notting Hill, a quiet residential district of London. Half way along on the right is the Greek Orthodox Church, known affectionately among many of the Greek community as the 'cathedral' of St Sophia. The church, sheltered behind a line of ilex trees, stands back from the street protected by a wrought-iron railing. On the other side of the road a mews trends away from the church in the general direction of the Bayswater Road.

Built by London's Greek community in the 1870's, the building, behind its evergreen oaks, at first sight is rather anonymous. On closer inspection, though, its Byzantine heritage is striking, and this becomes more evident as you enter the building for you find yourself lost in another world. The central feature of the interior, which dominates the entire structure, is the dome. It is spectacular.

Ben arrived early, a good half-hour before the service was due to start. A mixed group, mainly Greek but with a number of English, had already gathered in the small rectangular lobby leading to the main entrance. It was evident from the way they had grouped into small, loose clusters, and the easy nature of their conversation, that they were well known to each other. So much so that he felt a bit of an interloper. A notice to the left of the entrance – in English this one, unlike the others which were in Greek – issued the stark warning for such a holy place, it read *Attention Pickpockets – make sure you keep your personal belongings secure.* How thoughtful of them, it struck Ben, to warn pick-pockets that they should keep an eye on their belongings.

Only a few of the faces meant anything to him, probably those he'd seen during visits to the Greek Embassy off Holland Park. What suddenly caught his breath was to spot the man he had been talking about with Sue, the imposing figure of Leonides Androustes. At first he hadn't recognised him, for he was now a much-smartened up version of the Androustes he had met in Piraeus. He stood out from the crowd: a tanned face, hair brushed

13

back from his forehead in a single sweep and a kindly, patrician look all added up to the strong features of Leonides.

Altogether, a total of about thirty – mainly embassy – people, had turned up, Sue Karamanlis among them. Gill was not there yet, so far as he could see. Rather than hanging about and feeling conspicuous, he went in and found a seat in the spacious choir loft at the back of the church. Facing the altar, this enclave was well above ground level, like an open mezzanine. At eye level and directly in front was a large cross, hanging horizontally, with four quadrants of beautifully worked metal tracery holding as many as fifty oil lamps in red glass. It was impressive.

The internal surface of the dome was covered in gold-leaf, dominated by a mosaic showing Christ, arms uplifted in a gesture of welcome. Around the dome's base were mosaics of the twelve apostles with small, arched windows placed between each. Set into the floor immediately under the dome was the crown and double-headed eagle of the Byzantine Empire, an orb and sceptre in its claws. At this focal point, George's coffin had been placed on stools at each end.

Unlike the rows of pews found in churches, here there were rows of wooden stalls. Well spaced, they looked comfortable, each embellished by carvings on the back and on the arm rests.

By now, most of the congregation had taken their places. Gill was at the end of a row towards the back. Up in the eyrie of his choir loft, Ben had been joined by a handful of younger mourners and, seated unobtrusively in the corner, was a well-built man in a shiny suit. This man's hair was short almost to the point of baldness, and a thin scar ran down his left cheek towards his jaw. He had chosen a seat at the back of the choir area to keep himself out of sight. Taking in every detail, who was there and where they were seated, he appeared to be the sort of man who, either by training or instinct, would remember exactly what he had seen. Ben was sure that the man had taken in everything about him.

14

Sitting waiting for the service to begin, Ben came across a leaflet giving information about the Orthodox religion: that, as its name suggests, it had been the Orthodox Church that had preserved the true Christian faith in its original form, going its own way in the 9th century when a schism forced it to do so. He was disappointed to note that the leaflet failed to mention anything about priests and beards, that those with any serious ambition for promotion to patriarch would be required to grow nothing less than a rain forest of facial hair.

The funeral service was traditional, short and to the point, with no intermissions for special music, no anthem sung by a choir and no address. It was a solemn, deeply religious observance marking the end of a life. Amid this solemnity, Ben couldn't stop himself from wondering, just how poor George's life might actually have come to an end. He even began to wonder whether the man in the corner wearing a shiny suit might have played a part.

The rites of the funeral service ended, the final, hanging notes of supplication sung by the two chanting priests drawing it to a close. George's coffin was lifted onto the shoulders of the pall-bearers – stalwart men in late middle-age, grey haired, with weathered faces full of character – who bore the coffin slowly out of the church to the waiting hearse for its journey to the crematorium. Each person in the congregation was left to their own thoughts, most wearing faces that were well enough masked from giving their thoughts away.

It was time to join the main throng of mourners. As he turned to leave, Ben noticed that the man sitting attentively at the back had already gone.

Back at ground level, across the sea of faces in the nave, Ben spotted Gill. Not far from her stood the sinister man from his choir loft, chewing away at what could have been a nicotine sweet. He decided that this was not the moment to join her and went instead in search of Sue Karamanlis. It turned out that she, too, had been looking for him and was moving in his direction.

'We must meet.' she said breathlessly. Could you ring me at the embassy in an hour or so? Maybe we can catch a cup of coffee somewhere? Give me a call.' Seeing she was a bit flustered, Ben nodded and a second later she was gone.

Ben now had the opportunity to mix with the others, his first port of call being Andoustres. Surprised to see him, Leonides immediately leant over and gave him a crushing hug followed by a gentler pat on the back.

'Welcome to London,' said Ben recovering his breath, 'I'm sorry we meet like this.'

'Yes, my friend, so to me. But I pleased to see you. A sad business, no? I feared this might happen.'

Ben wasn't sure how to take this slightly elliptical comment, but sensed this was not the moment to pursue the matter. Could he, too, have known that George's life had been under some sort of threat?

'Where are you staying?'

'With Sue – Karamanlis that is' pausing briefly before adding 'and her husband.' He rolled his eyes in mock despair. 'She has gone to prepare a room for me. And to tell her husband!' He managed a shrug of his shoulders.

'As you're in my country can I return your hospitality – you were very generous when we met in Piraeus. With George, of course. Could you join us for dinner this evening?

'Bazili – Sue's husband – has a table at Korakis this evening, a Greek restaurant off the Marylebone Road. Why don't you join us? We can raise a glass to George.'

'Fine. I'll see if Gill can also come – she's just over there. I know she would like to meet you.'

Leonides followed Ben's gesture to where Gill was standing and with a fleeting smile nodded his approval. Then his brow furrowed, for he had seen the man standing near her, attentively talking with a well-dressed man, possibly from the embassy.

'Watch out him!' Leonides said gruffly, making an abrupt downward movement with his hand, as if to show how the man's face had been scarred. 'How you say, no good of a man? He stop nothing – even his own grandmother.'

The crowd was thinning, and it was clearly time to go. There was to be no wake, no party. Somehow it wouldn't have been appropriate, for George seemed to have no relatives, no immediate family, and his funds would probably not have run to a gathering of this many people in one of the nearby Bayswater hotels.

Ben went over to Gill to see if she was free for dinner, telling her that Sue Karamanlis and Androustes, and possibly others would be there. She jumped at the idea. He would call by her flat at seven to pick her up. With that sorted, he went through the big church doors and out onto Moscow Road. Having left his car on a meter in St Petersburg Mews, he crossed the road to take the turning almost opposite the church. There, half way down the Mews he could see it. He walked on.

5.

According to Ben's watch it was well past eight. Eight? He looked again, only to confirm what the watch had told him the first time. The first human being he saw was obviously a nurse, unmistakable in her crisp, blue and white uniform. This must, he thought, be some sort of hospital. It was, and he was on a stretcher, which was also a trolley, parked in what could only be a corridor. He pulled himself up for a better view. The nurse saw his movement and came over.

'How're you feeling?' she asked him, in the matter of fact way of nurses.

'Fine, well sort of.... but where am I?'

'In the Accident and Emergency at the Bayswater & General' she said. There could have been just a hint of an Irish lilt to her voice.

What? His head hinted at the answer. It ached, only slightly and at the back, but not so much that you would need to lie on a stretcher, he thought. The nurse looked deftly into his grey-blue eyes, turning his head a little to the right and left, and then from the left back to the right – sizing him up.

'Yes, you're doing well enough' she broke off before continuing 'you came off your bike over there in Bayswater, and if that wasn't enough it seems you banged your head on a lamppost. Concussed, you were. Not too badly, but enough.'

She seemed to know exactly what had happened. Yet as he listened, a problem sat immovably in the middle of her explanation – he didn't have a bike. Slowly, bits began to come back to him. He had been on his way from the church, walking down the mews to his car. Someone or something must have struck him from behind on the back of his head. And, now he came to think of it, yes, it may well have been a lamp-post that gave him such a heavy knock. He had a vague recollection of someone coming up behind him, quite fast. No more than that. But time was ticking by and he needed to phone Gill. She would be able to find the number of the *Korakis*, and ring through to say they couldn't make it. She might try to make a date for the following day. First, he had to find a telephone. With any luck the spirited young nurse could tell him where to find one. She did, and in a minute he was talking to Gill.

ooooooo

Quite used to her colleagues being unpunctual, Gill had put the time to good use getting through her list of things to be done, some quite pressing. Even so, she was relieved to hear from Ben though his story alarmed her. Was he really OK? Was he quite sure? Ben responded to the tone of solicitation in her voice and, yes, he reassured her, he was fine. As a matter of fact, they would be releasing him in less than half an hour. What would be just the ticket would be for her to grab a cab and pick him up from A & E before taking the cab on to his car not far up the road. It was obviously her turn to do the driving.

The duty doctor, having taken a look at Ben, pronounced him fit to leave. Looking at his notes he suggested it might be a kindness to call on the lady outside whose house he had had his fall. If it was on his way. It was Laura Wistanley and she had summoned the ambulance. He added that she was not only a celebrated pianist but also very pretty.

Gill showed up at the A&E reception, a flush of concern adding to the natural colour of her face. She thought Ben still looked a bit dazed, having the slightly puzzled look of someone who had just come out from the dentist. She took him by the arm and led him to the waiting taxi, asking the driver to take them on to St Petersburgh Mews.

As the taxi turned into the mews, Ben caught sight of his car. He could see it was still in one piece, and he rebuked himself for letting fanciful ideas flit across his mind. Then he noticed a parking ticket, stuck on the windscreen. He came back to earth with a bump, of a different sort this time.

No more than two yards behind his Audi, on the same side of the road, he noticed a lamppost, one of the stylish old wrought-iron ones from Victoria's reign, and leaning against it was a bike. On its chain-plate was the name Troubadour Chaser, slightly passé now, but not long ago it had been the mountain bike of choice. More telling, perhaps, he saw that it was tethered to the lamppost with a length of half-inch chain and a heavy pad-lock, both obscured from view by the basket on the handle-bars and the way the bike was leaning.

So that was how the mistake of riding a bike had come about – an easy enough error. The thought process from finding a man sprawled on the pavement by a bicycle to thinking he must have fallen off it was only logical. Such accidents were a common enough sight on the streets of any major city.

What should he do about Mrs Winstanley? Her house must be the one whose walls were trimmed with wisteria. Ben approached the latched wooden gate, which opened onto a tiled area in front of an ornate front door. A firm push of the door-bell and he stepped back. The lock turned and the door was edged back, revealing an elegant, middle-aged woman wearing an apron over a trouser suit. Trying to seem as relaxed as possible, he muttered hullo, while fumbling with his tie, realising as he did so that it was still the funeral black of that afternoon.

'Mrs Winstanley?' he asked.

'That's me.' she replied, arching a well-defined eye-brow enquiringly. Ben saw that the duty doctor was right, she was very good looking.

'I was given your name at the hospital. Apparently it was you who called the ambulance. I wanted to thank you and apologise for any trouble that I may have caused.'

'You needn't …' her voice trailed away, touched by his manner. Poised in the act of opening the door, her hand on her left hip, she could have been about to take a bow. 'Your friend said you'd fallen off your bike and hit your head.' She pointed in the direction of the lamppost.

'My f-friend?' a bit taken aback, he wasn't sure if he had heard her correctly.

'Well, the man who found you. He rang my door bell.'

'Oh, I see.' He didn't think he should question her version of the incident. 'He must have been passing by and stopped to help. You didn't get his name, by any chance?

'No,' she said, shaking her head. 'Like you' gesturing towards his neck 'he was wearing a black tie and he had a slight mark on his cheek.' she added, indicating her own cheek with an elegant finger.

It was time to move on. Ben, reaching into his pocket to give the car keys to Gill, found he also had a scruffy piece of paper in his hand. The writing on it though rough was clear enough – *kitaksi tin doulia sou.* Ben guessed it must mean 'Leave it out!' or something like that. He realised it must have been written by the fellow in the suit.

In the car, Gill told him she had managed to get through to Sue and they had made a date for lunch tomorrow, Leonides as well.

'Who was with you, Ben?' she had overheard the conversation with Mrs Winstanley.

Staring through the windscreen and thinking over his brief talk with the lady pianist, he wasn't clear how to put into words his understanding of what must have happened.

'No-one. I was on my own,' he said finally.

'She was wrong?'

'No, she just made the wrong assumption. She was supposed to. The man she thought must have been with me was someone I saw at George's funeral. You may have seen him…. An tough looking fellow in a shiny suit.'

He understood that what he faced now had become more serious. He must establish what the link was between George's death and the mystery of the painting. And, if he got really lucky, he might find out how the man in the suit fitted in.

Gill knew about the painting of course – though she had yet to see it – because Ben had described it to her.

'Let's go to the office and pick up the painting and take it back to my flat' said Gill, thinking ahead. 'It will only take a minute or two.'

The detour was worth it, if only to give him more time to collect his thoughts. From his office to Gill's flat was no great distance, and soon enough they were in her comfortable flat, surrounded by its collection of idiosyncratic furnishings. A Moroccan urn of great age and character dominated the spacious seating area, strewn with cushions and bric-a-brac bought at random on countless location trips.

Using a few of the large books on the coffee table to prop up the painting, they took a long, searching look at what was in front of them, and what they saw was a revelation. Hidden until that moment, the effect of the room's low lighting clearly hinted at a new dimension. For deadened by the lack of light, the central mass of colour had receded and instead the low side-lighting now revealed a previously unseen contour, the outline of a mountain, or perhaps just a shoulder. Ben wondered if it might just be the penultimate stage of *pentimento*, an Italian word meaning repentance – when an old painting shows itself through layers of paint that has been applied more recently; thus it is said to be repenting, allowing the glory of a former work on the original canvas to proclaim itself.

From whatever direction, the illusion of the emerging shape was sustained. Having walked back towards the door, Gill flicked the switch of the room's central light to see what effect more light would have on the canvas. It was dramatic: as she flicked the switch, the contour disappeared, instantly replaced by hurried brush strokes of gaudy paint. With the main light off once more, they found they were once again looking at the possible outline of a mountain.

Both were tired now, the only question being whose bed to fall into. In fact there was little contest, for when Gill shot a look in Ben's direction, he was already fast asleep on the sofa, deep in some sort of post-traumatic limbo. Two pillows and a duvet, she thought, would add much needed warmth and comfort.

6.

Ben was awake before dawn. His habit of waking early had started when he was a boy in Trinidad during the longer school holidays which he spent with his parents on the island. He simply hadn't wanted to miss a single second of the day. His father had been posted to Trinidad by the oil company he worked for to run the Antilles region, and Ben, who loved his time on the island was invariably the first to greet the dogs in the morning. That first hour was always exhilarating, and later at Oxford, while others along his corridor lay dozing or, more probably, dreaming of Sonia Frobisher's total disregard for modesty on the banks of the Isis, he would already have been up for an hour, reading. It was his time of day, and the 'early bird' in him used it well.

Ingrained habits die hard, and by six o'clock he was pacing around Gill's sitting room. No matter from what angle he viewed the painting he couldn't find a trace of the previous night's revelations. It wasn't his imagination, he knew it was the lighting, helped perhaps by impasto, a means of adding an extra dimension to a painting by building up layers of paint in particular areas often using a palette knife. The recollection of what he had seen was unshakable. The picture underneath would probably turn out to be a landscape, featuring a mountain in the centre background. The shape of the hill against the skyline didn't appear symmetrical, a disproportionately broad shoulder coming out on the right.

The more he thought about it – bearing in mind George's origins – the mountain was likely to be somewhere in Greece. His next guess was that it might be somewhere in the Peloponnese – George's home territory after all, where George said he was headed on his fateful journey.

A kettle began whistling in the kitchen. So he wasn't the only soul alive on planet earth - Gill too was alive and well. She soon came through the door towards him, bearing a cup of her morning elixir

– finely cut ginger over which, with a slice of lemon, she had poured boiling water.

'Morning, darling boy!' Affectionate, even protective, she was glad he was up. 'Here's some rocket fuel for you. How long have you been prowling about?'

'Quite a while.' Keen to talk about last night's discovery, Ben's words tumbled out quickly 'do have a look at this painting. In this light it just looks a mess.'.

Once again, as she flicked off the central light switch, the outline of the hill re-appeared, as if by magic.
'The mountain must be in Greece – probably in the Peleponnese. That was where George was headed.'

Ben recalled that the Peleponnese would have been an island had it not been for Corinth on the isthmus connecting it to the Greek mainland. Both Corinth and the Peleponnese had played a pivotal role in the ancient history of Greece. Although he couldn't be certain, he seemed to remember that somewhere along the east coast of the central finger – the shape of the Peleponnese vaguely resembled a dangling hand – there was a fishing village with a mythical history.

'Did you know that the entrance to Hades is in a village at the end of the middle finger of the Peleponnese? Spooky for those who live there…'

Good, she thought, he has obviously recovered.

'Ben,' she said, as though she had just been reminded of it 'don't forget we're having lunch with Sue today. As you suggested I booked a table for five at the Travellers – at a quarter to one.'

Ben had been a member there since his Godfather, who had been on the committee, had one day decided that Ben should start meeting people who wore a jacket and tie.

' I'm away to my flat for a shave and a change of clothes. And another tie, this is too black.' He looped his discarded tie towards the painting, like a cowboy lassoing a horse.

7.

Within the hour Ben had taken a shower and changed. Before leaving he reckoned there would be just be enough time to look at a map of Greece. Reaching for his atlas he turned to the page for Greece and there found the Peloponnese on a page all to itself. Yes, here was the land of myth and legend. His eye was immediately caught by the central 'finger', known as the Mani, a peninsula famous for its feuding clans and turbulent past. But then, which region of Greece wasn't? Scattered across the rest of the Peloponnese he also noticed the word Oros in bold type; thinking this must be the Greek for mountain he was left wondering which one. Bringing to mind the many other half-remembered details of this ancient part of Greece, he recalled thumbing through Thucidydes at school, wondering at the Spartan's insatiable appetite for carnage.

But time was passing, and he needed to be at the Travellers before the others. With his jacket half on, checking the pockets for his wallet and keys, he was out through the front door in one fluent movement headed for Pall Mall..

ooooooo

They arrived together, Gill leading the way. Ben had got as far as the library, an impressive room with an eye-catching frieze running around the top of the walls, copied from the temple at Bassae in Arcadia. A good omen, thought Ben.

Sue was looking elegant and business-like in a light cotton suit. She quickly apologised for her husband Bazili, who had been detained at the Embassy by visitors from Athens. Ben passed a message to say that they would only be four for lunch, as they occupied a cluster of comfortable club chairs by the window for a drink.

The conversation started naturally enough with observations about the funeral. What did Leonides make of it all? Looking thoughtful, he had so far been the quiet man of the party, with Sue shooting glances in his direction to reassure herself that he was fitting in. Ben felt he had to get Leonides to open up, to be more the man he had met nearly a year ago. He was a good-looking man, with a face made more beguiling by having just a hint of mischief flitting across his wide mouth. But it was his eyes that caught your attention. Black as coal, shining brightly, they looked as though they could penetrate steel. Ben guessed mentioning George might be a good way to get him going.

'Had George ever been married?' For a brief, dreadful moment Ben imagined he might actually have said murdered instead of married.

'I think so,' said Sue, turning to Leonides, 'but, Leo would know.'

'Yes, he was.' Almost the first time he had joined in, Leonides responded quickly. 'George was married to a young Athenian called Artemesia who sang an angel. He fell for her the moment they met. We all did. Being older, George was also a bit of a father figure - she thought the world of him. They were very happy'

'What happened?' Gill sensed a story.

'It was back in the time of the Colonels - the Junta - a time when for their own good most people pretended to know nothing.' The older man's mood had changed and he spoke with strong distaste. 'One day she disappeared and it was assumed she must have done something the regime didn't approve of. Easy make Junta angry. Remember? They say not long hair for men, not short skirts for womens! She disappeared. Gone. Much happened in 1970. George blame

28

himself. For six months he like a dead man. Then, one day, he up and left Athens to London and never said of her again.'

Leonides had come alive, evidently feeling nothing but loathing for the Colonels. His eyes gleamed with remembrance of long forgotten passions held during those difficult days. He didn't find English all that easy, though he was able to get by without being too much at a loss. Like most Greeks he rolled his 'r's and resorted to clearing his throat when pronouncing his 'h's. It added to the charm of his speaking voice.

'George a cousin of mine, h'is father my father were brothers. When young, we also like brothers.'

This news came as a surprise to them, though Sue must have known that George and he were related in some way.

Ben decided that the time had come to move into the dining room. Frequently overlooked, one of the advantages of a club over a restaurant is that there is space between the tables, and they were doubly fortunate in the table they were given because it was tucked away in the corner. Another advantage is that you can stick with the same choice of food once you have discovered what they do well. Whitebait followed by liver and bacon was a safe bet, and Gill got the meal off to a good start by again lobbing in a seemingly innocent question.

'Did you know that George had left Tom a painting?'

'No,' Leonides was genuinely surprised, 'not an El Greco?' Briefly lost to the others, he wheezed away at his own little joke.

'I think we need another bottle!' Ben smiled 'Yes, of course it was some sort of a *Greco*, it had to be, it was by George himself.'

'But he didn't paint,' objected Leonides 'he not know one end of brush from other, except the one for his hair.'

'Well,' Gill interjected 'he left instructions with us, that is my film company, to send the painting round to Tom after he took off on his last trip.'

Speaking quietly and clearly, she was looking directly at Leonides who had instantly become keenly interested. Ben took up the running and recounted the arrival of the painting.

'Signed GA in the bottom corner, I assumed the painting was George's. You might like to see it, after lunch perhaps.'

The conversation returned to George. According to Leonides, his and George's ancestors had really been brigands, belonging to one of the country clans known as Klephts. They provided an all-important constituent of a secret brotherhood known as the *Filiki Eteria,* formed in 1814 to promote revolution against the Ottoman Turks. In fact, the Klephts had taken to the mountains much earlier, not long after the Turkish conquest.

'Klephts aren't the same as Klephtomaniacs?' said Ben, mock horror on his face.

'Same word in Greek, *kleptes* means thief.' There was a note of pride in his voice.

Apparently they had a fearsome reputation, well earned, for swooping down from the fastness of their lairs in the hills and plundering for food, and anything else that might come in handy like your daughter or your wife. Heavily armed with swords, rifles and daggers, they wore raffish clothes and had wonderful moustaches as wide as aeroplane wings.

Time had passed quickly and the dining room was beginning to empty. Sue said she had to get back to the embassy, leaving the three of them to walk to Gill's flat.

oooooo

Mercifully it was tidy. There, perched on the coffee table in the middle of the room, stood the picture, propped up by a pile of books. It was an awkward moment, no-one knowing where to begin. In front of them, after all, was nothing more than a splurge of colour. Striding over to the door Gill turned off the overhead light. The effect was instantaneous. There, for all of them to see, was something very like the outline of a mountain.

Leonides was electrified. Moving forward, he canted his head from side to side trying to identify the shape, delving for clues. Finding nothing, he ran his fingers over the centre area, enticing it to yield more. But it didn't. Giving up, he changed tack and pointing at the initials in the bottom right hand corner said:

'Initials, GA, are George,' he said, 'they how he signed name, same backward flourish of A. The 'A' of course originally for Androustes,' he added as if stating the obvious, 'Georgios Androustes the name he was born with.'

Though clearly intrigued by what he had seen, Leonides was not the kind of man to give his feelings away. His mind had moved on to a linked thought, which he was trying to put into the right words. Adopting the portentous tone of an uncle addressing nephews he started by saying:

'Embassies all over the world have people called advisers, men and women with special knowledge or training. Sometimes, just spies. Well, George no spy – he cultural adviser, more like

31

British Council. Hellenism his subject – the signature of all things Greek.'

Very Greek, and probably more complex than anyone could possibly imagine, thought Ben. During the never-ending occupation of Greece by the Ottoman Turks, the general *diaspora* of Greeks had been continuous. Away from their homeland many had prospered, remitting funds home through the Orthodox Church for education, keeping the spirit of Hellenism alive. However, there was no escaping the fact that from time to time grim atrocities had been committed, and it should not be a surprise to learn that the duty of revenge had been kept high on the agenda of many warring families.

Mulling over what Leonides had just said, Ben understood exactly what he meant. George was widely known among the Greek community, and he would certainly have had connections at many levels of government during the era of the Colonels, the time of his wife's mysterious disappearance. Thinking more about George and his contacts, the *fogs* in his note-book, Ben realised that George must have lead a very complicated life. Possibly someone with a score to settle might have been behind the episode on the ferry? Headed for the Peloponnese, George was on a visit that was surely more than a holiday. And Ben knew that he feared for his safety.

8.

After an unmistakably clear hint from Gill, Ben knew they must act. She said she really couldn't go on listening to any more theorising - or dithering as she saw it - and insisted they get in touch with a restorer. They needed practical guidance on resurrecting a painting and they needed it urgently.

Next morning Ben phoned a friend of his sister's, Giles Gallande. He had been at the St Martins School of Art with her, and since then had also become a good friend of Ben's.

Giles had a growing reputation as a portrait painter, though pretty well every aspect of painting clearly fascinated him, spending hours discussing techniques and technicalities with anybody who would listen. At one stage he had had a fixation with what he called the concept of depth, quoting the experience of looking into a pond at familiar objects: the changed perspective given by depth, made the objects appear to be in altered relationships with each other. Neither Ben nor his sister was quite sure if they had grasped the full meaning of the pond concept, it all seemed too murky.

Giles wasn't there, but a girl's voice told Ben he'd only gone out to get some yoghurt and would be back in a few minutes. In no time Giles was on the phone, firing off questions at his friend Benbow as though he was a private investigator.

'How goes it?' his voice was full of energy. Giles always enjoyed the cut and thrust of a chat with Ben - he often had a fresh angle on most subjects.

.

'I need to talk to you about a painting,' Ben quickly got to the point 'an oil painting, given to me a few days ago. I think it could have been over-painted.'

Though Giles didn't immediately catch Ben's drift, he sensed his urgency, getting straight to the point. He let him continue.

'I was left the painting by a colleague who died recently' continued Ben, instinctively knowing hat this was not the moment to complicate matters by explaining his growing suspicions.

'One of the reasons I think it must have been over-painted, is that it looks quite dreadful. I'd love to know what may be lurking underneath. Do you know of a reliable restorer?'

'I do. But why don't I take a look at it?'

'Even better. But when?' Ben pressed hopefully.

'I'm rather stuck on a portrait. She's outrageously beautiful and I'm finding it nearly impossible to concentrate. So I could even come round now, a break would be welcome. You have the painting?'

'No, I don't. It's in Gill's flat. We can walk round there. See you in a minute.' Ben put down the phone and called Gill to warn her.

As good as his word, Giles was soon standing at the door of Ben's apartment and next to him was a strikingly attractive companion. She was an Indonesian. Known to her friends as The Siphon, a childish mispronunciation of her real name, Sifonia, she was beautiful with a smile as warming as a rising sun. The three of them strolled round to Gill's place, making up for lost time with the inevitable banter of old friends who had a lot of catching up to do.

Gill welcomed them. She had been aware of Ben's friend for a long time and had always wanted to meet him. Leading the way into the sitting room she lifted the painting off its perch and handed it to Giles. The first thing he did was to turn it round and look at the back.

'As you say, this outer bit, the decorative framing is obviously not new, made from what looks like olive wood. Just take a look at the dove-tailing at the corners; that sort of workmanship hasn't gone into a frame for years.'

Showing a keen professional interest, Giles spoke with the ease and fluency of a man who really knew his subject.

'The painting itself is on stretched canvas' he went on, closely examining the stretcher where the keys and wedges held the inner frame together. 'As far as I can tell the canvas has been lined at least once, which would suggest that it, too, is old, a couple of hundred years perhaps.'

Giles, well into his stride, had turned the painting round to scrutinise the front.

'Yes, this has had paint sloshed all over it, and quite recently. Probably acrylic whose chief property, as you know, is that it dries quickly. Easy enough to remove so long as the painting underneath isn't cracked. It could turn out to be a landscape, a view of the Highlands, that sort of thing. The shape gives it away. But too small for a Landseer, I'm afraid!'

Ben nodded. Could they find the right person to clean it, someone who could restore the painting to its original condition? Ben was about to ask, but Giles, reading his mind, cut in with a suggestion he simply could not refuse.

'I could clean it. But if the painting is of any importance, I would be happier if it went to Cedric. He does restoration work for all the museums.'

Giles paused, remembering one or two of Cedric Simmonds's more endearing idiosyncrasies. A bit of a romantic, he was given to fantasising about life on board the old sailing ships, often falling back on the colourful language of the days of the old tea clippers to add a bit of drama to a story. He turned to Ben.

'Cedric is the man for this - very much his cup of tea. I'll ring him. Meanwhile, I'll take your precious artwork back to my studio. There's some preliminary work I could get on with - it would save Cedric a lot of time.'

' Great' said Ben 'I hope your man won't take for ever. We need to know what lies underneath these awful colours with some urgency.'

He felt this was hardly the moment to tell Giles about the succession of curious events that had started with the arrival of the picture, including the harrowing episode after George's funeral.

'I have a hunch this painting,' Ben pointed at the mass of gaudy colours 'is supposed to be telling us something. A message of some sort. George,' he broke off to emphasise the point 'George was probably in a panic brought on by fear. In the event of anything nasty happening to him, he wanted to pass the painting on to someone else, to be sure of relaying its message. And he chose to cover the canvas, to hide, well, whatever he felt needed to be hidden.'

The four of them sat back, with a heightened sense of curiosity. Although restorers were known to be a fussy, fastidious breed - inclined to caution by nature, and painstakingly slow workers - Giles said he would push Cedric to make sure he didn't take for ever.

Half an hour later Ben watched the mysterious painting being bundled into a black cab, sandwiched between Giles and his beautiful friend. He hoped it would not be long before Giles had something to show him.

9.

Cedric lived in Greenwich, up a street leading away from the river. His large flat, to a charitable eye, looked chaotic; to a less forgiving one it looked more like a crime scene, the only thing missing being the blue and white police tape. To be fair, his sitting room often doubled as his workshop. On a busy day bottles of liquids, some of them quite lethal, would be scattered around the room. Bottles littered the tables, others stood like sentinels on the floor and yet more were perched on the sills of the windows.

When the summons came from Giles, he reacted immediately. Emergencies appealed to his sense of drama, a repressed yearning for adventure. He reached down an old airline bag, into which he placed a partitioned wooden box containing four small vials of chemicals. To these he added a selection of plastic containers and a roll of what looked like paint brushes. Not forgetting his wallet, he also tossed into the bag a small electrical apparatus resembling a hair dryer. Seizing an old Breton sailor's cap, a cherished possession, he was off to the pier and through to the Jubilee Line. As promised, he was walking up the stairs to Giles's second floor studio within the hour.

'Ahoy!' he bellowed to all the landlubbers in the room as he stepped through the studio door. He went on to say that in his experience it was best to be brutal with acrylic.

'The oil paint underneath will of course have set pretty solid over the years and will come to no harm. Just grab the acrylic by the throat and give it a good swabbing' he was addressing Giles without even a glance in his direction. In reality he was talking to himself. 'We should start on the edge of the canvas, where the acrylic will be thinnest and where we can hope to find a good range of colours, we'll then be able to see how to proceed. Why don't I get started right away?'

The canvas had already been taken out of its frame and had been placed on an easel near the window to get the best of the natural light. Cedric seized it firmly and placed it flat on its back on the nearest table; it had to be level to inhibit the liquids from running. First he took out an old paint-brush handle, around which he wound cotton wool. Then, reaching deeper into his bag he drew out what he called a safety bottle, a small aluminium container with a sprung lid, which he could open and shut with a flick of his thumb. He gave it a shake and set to work.

In what seemed like no time at all some of the acrylic had been removed and a small section of the painting underneath was becoming visible. Cedric took a step back to see how it was going. All was well.

'As expected, the acrylic is coming away very easily, causing no problems,' the observation needing no reply, he went on 'and as far as I can tell the old painting which is beginning to show itself is going to need a bit of cleaning, perhaps some restoration.'

A thorough cleaning would necessarily be a methodical, time-consuming process. He paused thoughtfully for a moment before turning to Giles to say that he would concentrate on removing the acrylic first, until most of that was history. After that they could stand back and take a good look at the whole painting and then decide what to do. Before moving on to that next stage he would need to experiment with different agents and solvents. Taking another, closer look at the edge of the canvas on the stretcher, he confirmed what Giles had said, that the painting had been lined twice.

He fell silent as he set to work. Using short circular movements of the brush handle over the surface of the canvas, he frequently dipped it and its cotton wool padding into the safety bottle, flicking the hinged lid open and shut with practised fluency. The little aluminium bottle contained a mixture of ethanol and water, and he began by dabbing the fluid onto to a test area near the edge, gradually working his way towards the centre. From time to time he discarded the paint-stained cotton wool and wound a fresh piece round the brush handle. He was meticulous. Nothing could make him hurry, lost in his own world.

The truth was that each time he started to clean an old painting Cedric couldn't resist a gentle onrush of adrenaline. It was always the same – a keen shimmer of excitement at the prospect of uncovering something of consequence, should he ever get to be so lucky. He guessed that the painting must be getting on for a hundred and fifty or more years old, which would make it early Victorian. As he continued with his circular brushing he couldn't help running through a few of the better-known names from the period. No harm in that, certainly no worse than listening to the radio. Uncovering a Constable or a Turner would be the high spot of anyone's career; and, in his case, it would be like winning the jackpot, enabling him to realise his dream of buying a boat studio on Chelsea Reach. All of that was absurdly fanciful, but so what? These were only the private thoughts of a mild romantic as he delved away.

The task of removing the freshly applied layer of paint was going according to plan. As he progressed, he mopped up the liquefied acrylic with cotton wool, section by section, working in towards the centre with deft hand movements. Slowly the painting, so urgently concealed by George Abbott, was once more beginning to see the light of day.

It was three hours since he had taken off his jacket, yet in that time the bulk of the newly applied acrylic had been removed, making it possible to begin to see the composition as a whole. It was still messy, but at least the subject matter of the original had now become clear.

'That'll do!' growled Cedric, 'For now.'

Getting up from his chair, he wiped his hands on the cloth tucked into his belt like a waiter. Giles, taken aback by Cedric's sudden Rottweiler-like outburst, put down his own brushes and walked over to the window to get a better view. He was able to see immediately that the old salt from Greenwich had worked wonders.

That it was a landscape was now clear; and, yes, the main feature was a mountain. And judging by the absence of strong colour across the somewhat barren landscape, it seemed to Giles that it might be some sort of limestone massif. Whoever had painted it had indeed resorted to *impasto*, adding layers of paint within the area of the mountain itself to bulk it up. Reading Giles's mind Cedric piped up to say that since *impasto* hadn't come in much before 1800, might that help to date the picture? Giles quickly nodded in affirmation.

While some sections were still obscured by smears of acrylic, the main section of the foreground was beginning to show interesting detail, emerging as the focal point of the composition. The definition of each shrub, each tree, each contour of the land had been caught quite beautifully by the artist. The landscape, though on a grand scale, was by no means just shrubs, trees and rocks. In the lower middle section there were some carefully rendered old buildings – possibly cattle sheds or outhouses. And immediately below these there was something white, possibly a cross. It was hard to tell.

Cedric again delved into his bag, this time producing the hair dryer. In fact, it was a U/V light, the rays casting a yellowish glow over the section of the painting it was aimed at. Wearing the right

41

sort of sun-glasses, you were able to see whether a more recent layer of paint had been applied. It was still too early to tell.

Giles pulled the cork from a bottle of chilled sauvignon-blanc then stretched his legs over the arm of the studio sofa. He wasn't entirely sure about the newly revealed painting.

'Here's to you, you old magician!' he raised his glass to Cedric 'To the ultra-violet art of seeing lost paintings!'

Taking a sip he came to the conclusion that the picture might just be a tad boring. After another sip, and being scrupulously fair, he thought that something so obviously well painted might grow on him. The time had come to ring Ben.

10.

Giles welcomed Ben to the madhouse that his studio was fast becoming and introduced him to Cedric. Ben immediately warmed to Cedric, finding him a congenial man with a sense of humour - definitely a kindred spirit. Ben also noticed that he had quaint mannerisms, realising that he might turn out to be a bit of an eccentric. They both went over to the window to take a look at the recently revealed artwork. For a minute or two Ben was at a loss for words.

'We guessed it would be a mountain, and we can now see that it is a huge one. But where is it?' asked a bewildered Ben.

He needed time to catch up with the others who had seen the results of Cedric's cleaning emerge more gradually. Even so, he felt a bit disappointed. The painting was lying on its back on the table where Cedric had left it to dry, making it hard for Ben to understand the finer points of the canvas, and since there appeared to be no obvious explanation for what had so far come to light, Ben felt vaguely let down by the result and was beginning to wonder if it wouldn't just be better to call it a day. But Cedric piped up.

'You see this hill, mountain, call it what you will. It is north facing. I mean, see how the shadows fall, particularly where there are buildings here in this lower section. They all fall in the same direction, down the slope. Presuming the painting is in the northern hemisphere, the shadows suggest that north is roughly here.'

He pointed, more or less back towards the empty easel, now behind them, the unstable tripod of its legs having taken several knocks as people approached the table. Ben immediately grasped his meaning.

Feeling the first rays of hope returning, like the first shaft of sunlight at dawn, he saw there could be more. For judging by the short length of the shadows, the painting had to be a long way south, well south of the British Isles. Prompted by looking at shadows and their association with time, he looked up at the clock on the mantelpiece to see how much longer he would be able to stay. Turning towards the clock, his eye was caught by something else. He registered – he should have noticed it earlier – that the painting had been removed from its frame, giving Cedric a much better access for cleaning. The frame had been placed facing downwards on the sideboard near the fireplace. But what had caught his eye was a narrow piece of paper wedged into the recess of the frame, until now covered by the painting. Leaning over he found it was no larger than a cigarette paper, yellowed with age, and inscribed in the centre was a single Greek letter. A circle with a vertical line through it, that was all. It was the Greek capital Phi. Did Φ stand for something? Mysterious, thought Ben, placing it in his wallet.

Growing more intrigued by the minute, he remained where he was in front of the recently revealed landscape, hearing a distant echo of George's note - *you'll know what to do*. So far the emergence of a mountain had given him no clear line to follow up. Imagining that the painting had a message, logically what he was looking at must somehow show the message. The central feature, the mountain, the composition of the painting as a whole, these had been chosen to give a context for that message. But surely there was more to it than that?'

Meanwhile Cedric had been peering at the little white object in the centre of the painting, his face quite close to the canvas, deep in concentration. He stood back.

'As I said, all these shadows indicate that north is about there.' Once more, pointing behind him. 'But take a look at this little white cross, if that's what it is. Its shadow is falling in a quite different direction to all the other shadows everywhere else, the shadow line of the cross was clearly defined.'

Was it pointing to something, to a feature of significance, as a finger post points to a destination? Ben understood what Cedric was getting at; there was no doubt that whoever had painted the picture wanted you to understand that the position of the little white cross was crucial.

That the mountain had to be somewhere in Greece, Ben felt pretty certain. But that didn't help much because there were almost as many mountains in Greece as there were bottles of retsina. From Homer's citadel cliffs to Byron's mountains of Marathon, there were mountains, mountains everywhere. And the picture might just be of a completely fictitious mountain, an imagined landscape plucked from the dusty shelf of mythology. To discover its whereabouts– if it existed at all– might take a bit of doing, but it had to be done, it must be his priority. Hadn't George Abbott gone out of his way to say that no-one had a better instinct? That he would know what to do? He had better get on and do it then.

○○○○○○

Ben remembered Leoonides saying that the outline reminded him of Mount Parnassus. If so, that should be easy to check. Asking Giles if he could use his phone, he called the Greek Embassy asking to be put through to Sue Karamanlis. She stopped him almost immediately, saying that Androustes had caught the plane back to Athens before lunch.

'You've just missed him, Ben. But can I help?' Her enquiry was polite, perhaps not only out of a desire to help, but also because her diplomatic training had prompted her to find out what it was that Ben was delving into.

'Well, maybe you can' he said quickly. 'I'm looking for

45

someone who can help me identify Mount Parnassus. A climber, a skier perhaps, a photographer – someone who knows the area.'

'I can do better than that.' she replied. 'Just off the foyer in the main entrance of the Embassy, down the corridor to the left of the reception desk, there is a large painting of Parnassos. It's by Vryzakis, famous for his record of the Revolution, what we call the War of Independence. It could be just what you're looking for. Drop round tomorrow morning at about eleven o'clock. I'll make sure you can look at it for as long as you like. No-one will think you're about to steal it – it's too big!

oooooo

Ben had other calls on his time. His consultancy had been invited by one of the agencies in Brussels to submit a plan for assessing investment levels of sections of the European metal industry. It sounded like a re-run of the Iron and Steel Federation but Ben knew better than that; it had more to do with what they called metal derivatives like aluminium. Much of the preliminary work had been done, and in a month their proposals had to be finalised and ready for presentation. He and his partner, Mike, had to find time for a preliminary run through their recommendations.

Despite it being late he telephoned finding Mike still in the office. Grateful to hear from Ben, he quickly took him through the main points of the work in progress, adding a plea from Ben's PA to say that she wasn't a mind reader, so could he please risk breaking radio silence and make contact with her as she had dozens of messages. Getting quickly to the point, Ben suggested they meet: how about a drink this evening?

'Better first thing tomorrow, if that suits. I'm late as it is. Let's meet for a coffee tomorrow morning, say eight o'clock at our coffee shop by the office. And Ben,' said Mike 'there's one quick thing you should know … hang on, no, look Ben, I think there may be someone here. It can wait till I see you in the morning. See you at eight. Bye.' He was gone.

Ben had other things to occupy him and didn't give much thought to Mike's rather abrupt ending of their conversation. He must ring his PA, and calm her down.

oooooo

Just before eight o'clock the following morning, Ben was perched on a stool in their coffee shop, inadvertently distributing bits of croissant all over the floor. It was going to be a busy day.

Knowing that Mike took every opportunity for exercise seriously, he would be riding his bike the six miles or so from home to the office; apart from the exercise it was quicker. But Mike was late. And after another twenty minutes, there was still no sign of him. Ben decided to call him at home.

'Hullo?' came more an enquiry than an answer, from Mike's wife, Maureen.

'Hi there.' said Ben gently 'I'm supposed to be meeting Mike for a coffee at eight, but he's nowhere to be seen. Any idea where he might have gone?'

A silence from the other end of the line, finally broken by a less hesitant Maureen as she found her voice. Apparently Mike had, as she described it, taken a bit of a tumble the previous evening on the office stairs. He had strained an ankle quite badly in the fall. Maureen went on to say that he was hobbling about but expected to be more mobile by tomorrow. if it could wait he would call Ben back then.

Shit! Ben muttered to himself. How on earth did he manage that? It didn't sound all that serious, and yes, it could wait.

oooooo

Ben decided to park his car in the Avenue behind Holland Park where there was a free meter. The short walk would give him a chance to organise his thoughts before seeing Sue. He could do with the exercise. Poor Mike! How had that happened? He hardly ever had a drink, so what was he doing falling down the stairs? He must ring the office. But first, he would take a look at the picture in the embassy.

The rhythm of walking induced just the right kind of calming, *solvitur ambulando* as it was known. It helped clear the brain, and his brain needed clearing. Soon he would be in the embassy looking at a painting of Parnassos; hopefully he would then get a clear indication of whether his mountain was Parnassus or not. Of course Parnassos was to the north of the Gulf of Corinth, so any lingering thoughts he still entertained about the Peloponnese would be dashed.

11.

The dark-haired girl on the reception desk of the Greek Embassy
had beautifully manicured nails. These clicked on the buttons of
an elaborate computer keyboard in front of her, reminding Ben of
the sound made by one of those fabled African tribes, the *Xhosa*,
who communicate with each other by clicking their tongues on the
roof of their mouths. She got through to Sue Karamanlis, listened
intently, then nodded her understanding of what she should do
with the visitor eagerly studying her every movement from the
other side of her desk. She turned to Ben.

'The picture you've come to see is that one' the tone and clarity
of her voice was perfect as she pointed towards a sort of alcove
or corridor to her left. Tom could just make out the corner of
a large heavy gilt frame. 'Mrs Karamanlis said to take as long
as you like – she will be down to join you when she can get
away.'

Her serious face broke into a welcoming smile, cascading charm
all over Ben. A good start, he thought. Such magnificent teeth!
Reluctant to leave the zone of warmth and possibility in the
vicinity of the gorgeous receptionist, he forced himself away and
walked slowly across the foyer in the direction she had indicated.

Looking up at the huge painting he found himself staring in open
disbelief; it was very similar to the one George had left him,
nearly the same except much, much bigger, a near replica, though
on a very much larger scale. Some obvious differences that Ben
spotted immediately: for instance, there were no buildings in the
painting in front of him, not a single one.

A frisson of excitement permeated his whole body. At last! He was
getting somewhere. The small, carved plaque attached to the base
of the elaborate frame, stated that it was Mount Parnassus. The

small plaque also said that it had been painted by someone called Theodoros Vryzakis, with the dates (1814 – 1878) in brackets after his name.

Was the similarity between the paintings just a coincidence? Or was there more to it than that? Was there something special about the north face of this mountain that he was unaware of? Just then, he sensed the presence of someone standing quite close to him. He turned to find Sue.

'Hi,' she greeted him like a long lost friend, 'now you've seen it, what do you make of our mountain?' Her intonation, though frivolous, also sought an explanation.

'Fascinating' said Tom 'It's Parnassus, the same as my picture, which as far as I'm concerned confirms its identity.' He wanted Sue to tell him some more about Vryzakis.

'One of Greece's better-known painters,' she said with some pride 'famous for his paintings of the period, the era immediately following our liberation from the Turks. His father died during the Revolution, and I believe that was why he became so emotionally involved with this period of our history. One of his most famous paintings depicts the blessing of the Flag of Independence - at Agia Lavra, an old monastery in the Peleponese - a painting that helped the monastery to become symbolic of the actual start of the movement that led to Greece's freedom.

'The flag we know today?'

'No. It was only a pale blue cross on a white background.'

Her voice had become almost dreamy, as though while recalling the event the nostalgia of the moment had seeped into her.

'Many of Vryzakis's paintings are romantic, and most of them tell a story. But the details of dress and location in all his works are always recorded very accurately.'

Facing the landscape again, Ben felt an urge to point out where the similarities ended.

'Though both paintings have much in common,' he said 'there are in fact minor differences. Towards the bottom of your painting, here for example, there aren't any buildings.' He waved his hand across the canvas, hovering over the lower section to emphasise where the missing buildings were.

'Oh,' she said, realising she had caught up with an important development rather late in the day 'your picture has been cleaned?

'Nearly, there's just a little more to be done.'

' But you said houses?' she persisted, turning a quizzical gaze on him.
'Down here,' again he moved his hand over the lower area 'not houses, just a few old old sheds.' Ben began to wonder if he should have mentioned them at all.

'Perhaps it might be more rewarding to see what features the paintings have in common.' he continued, carefully steering the subject away from houses. 'You see, in many ways they are identical. They both show the same north facing slope, the same sort of vegetation, the same shoulder here' he pointed to the ridge on the right 'and the same dark splodge up here in the centre.'

'Oh, that!' she said picking up his reference to the dark area. Pointing at it herself she continued 'It isn't a splodge. That patch is a famous cave known as the *Mavre Troupe*. It means *Black Hole*.'

'The only Black Hole I know was in Calcutta during the 1857 Indian mutiny.' said Ben. It struck him for the first time since they had met that she was looking much more attractive.

'No reason why it should,' Sue replied, pushing her dark hair behind her ear 'the cave was once the headquarters for a band of freedom fighters during War of Independence. I believe it also had some sort of connection with your Lord Byron, though I don't think he ever went there. By the way, Bazili, my husband, originally came from the region near Parnassos. From time to time he has to go back there – some sort of business takes him back there.

Ben wondered how much he should tell Sue about the restoration of George's painting. He wondered why the paintings were so similar, yet not quite the same? He needed to see his own version again while the Vrysakis version was still fresh in his mind.

'There's something else' Sue went on 'that might be of interest to you. It's Leonides: whenever he comes to London he usually finds time to visit the Embassy, and not always to see his old friends: he likes to look at this picture. He seems to be intrigued by it.'

Interesting, thought Ben. Why should he be so keen to see this painting? How could he find out more, without alerting Sue? Perhaps he should hop on a plane to Athens? On reflection, that might alert Leonides, though he wasn't sure if that would matter. But Ben was beginning to see a way forward: he just needed a little more time to sort out the meaning of these recent discoveries, above all why was Parnassos the key to George's message?

'Good grief! Just look at the time,' he said, reluctant to leave Sue, who still showed every sign of wanting to be friendly 'it's nearly half past twelve and I have a lunch date. I must get going. Thanks for letting me see your mountain, Sue. It's been very interesting.'

Leaning forward to give her a kiss, to his surprise they met half way and she kissed him warmly, full on the mouth, gently slipping her arm inside his jacket.

'Why don't you and I have lunch one of these days?', she added meaningfully.

12.

Ben hurried from the leafy calm of Georgian Holland Park towards Giles's studio. Stimulated by the generous warmth of her kiss, his mind turned to imagining what the intimacy of love-making with her might be like, coming to the conclusion that it might be quite demanding. He wondered why her attitude towards him had changed, what had prompted her to become openly so suggestive? Anyway, she had certainly come through with a good result on Parnassos - and an offer for a bite of lunch. Ben almost blushed.

The similarity between the two paintings and the fact that Leonides was intrigued by the the painting in the embassy were questions clamouring for an answer. It was clear to him that either Leonides had to pay another visit to London, or he would have to go to Athens.

The studio was buzzing with life. The excitement in Cedric's corner had somehow seeped across the large room to where Giles was putting the finishing touches to his portrait of Siphonia. The brightness and colour of her exotic clothes had added sensation to beauty, and a recent visitor to the studio had told Giles that if he ever wanted to be judged as a painter, this had to be the painting he should be judged by.

Ben, waving to everyone as he slipped beneath the arched entrance to the studio, quickly headed in the direction of Cedric. The restorer was standing by the window, wondering whether it was too early for a brandy and ginger ale.

'I've just seen,' Ben was nearly shouting, his voice hardened by urgency 'a near duplicate, though on a very, very much larger scale.' Looking keenly at their painting, he went on 'It was in the Greek Embassy. But there was a major difference: there

54

wasn't a single building in the Embassy painting. Not one.' he was pointing at the lower right hand corner.

'That doesn't entirely surprise me' said Cedric, not fazed by Ben's outburst 'because I've been running over the outline of these buildings carefully. As you know, this u/v light shows up subsequent applications of paint. Well, all these buildings have been added and I would guess a long time ago for the image has faded.'

'Not part of the original?

'No. Hard to be a hundred percent sure, but it looks as though the sheds have been worked in later. You can see what I mean easily enough, just pop on these specs and shine the light over this first building.'

Ben put on the sort of dark-glasses Cedric was offering him and switched on the lamp. He was right. There was a dimmed luminescence around each of the buildings, not a millimetre beyond. They had been added.

The details of trees and shrubs in both paintings were the same; the shoulder running outwards from the centre and of course the brooding *cave*, all those details were clearly the work of the same painter. But it was no ordinary landscape: there was something uncanny about the artist's sensitivity to his surroundings: in the end he had produced a finished result of electrifying intensity, almost insisting that the viewer shouldn't see it as just simple mountain scenery.

George's painting was so similar that it also must be the work of Vryzakis. But though he might well have painted the original, thanks to Cedric it was becoming clear that a later hand had been at work.

'And don't forget the white cross, or whatever it is.' Cedric's voice without growing louder had become more emphatic. 'My guess is that it was the very last detail to be added to the canvas. It wasn't just put there haphazardly: the cross was placed in its position with extreme care, as was its shadow.'

Cedric ended with something of a flourish, his fingers flapping about over the relevant area of the painting, like gulls over scraps of fish. He had a point.

But Ben Benbow had other, more immediate, concerns. For the last few minutes he had been over by the window talking on the studio phone. It was obvious that something was troubling him, for when he rejoined Cedric his face showed the unmistakable pallor of disturbing news; and that he didn't feel like sharing this news with anyone in the studio was also easy to see. Not until he knew how to deal with what he had just heard. He badly needed fresh air. And he needed to call Gill.

Ben had been on the 'phone to Mike, who was quickly regaining his mobility by hopping about. One might even say, he thought mischievously, that he was getting better by leaps and bounds. It turned out that he hadn't fallen down the stairs. The cleaner, Lily Franks, has come across him in Ben's room in some agony. Apparently Mike, hearing unfamiliar noises coming from Ben's office, had gone round to find out what was going on. There he had encountered a man rifling through Ben's filing cabinets and the two large wooden racks used for storing flow charts. As soon as he entered, the intruder made a bolt for the door, knocking Mike off balance as he sped past him. He had fallen, catching his ankle awkwardly on the edge of the cabinet by the door. Mike added that he would recognize him again if he saw him: he had a mark on his cheek. It was this snippet of news that had disturbed Ben.

It hadn't been a botched burglary; it hadn't been a burglary at all. It was that sinister man, once again, this time rummaging about in his office. Where did he fit in, where was he from? He wasn't a cat, he didn't have nine lives, so he was running out of time as far as Ben was concerned. Popping up unexpectedly from time to time, he had to be someone's agent, someone's paid hand. Though Ben couldn't be sure, his hunch was that the 'someone' must have something to do with the embassy. The motive behind the actions of this man were now crystal clear: he was desperate to get his hands on the painting George had bequeathed him.

13.

When he came into the room Ben had the look of someone who had just seen a ghost - his face was expressionless and he was much quieter than usual.

Quickly he took Gill through the day's developments – the embassy picture and the worrying news from Mike about the reappearance of the man with a scar. Gill agreed that the connection had to be somebody at the embassy. How many of the embassy staff did they actually know? Not that many, when they stopped to think about it, only a handful like Sue and Bazil Karamanlis.

Running over the conversation he had had with Mike, he should have known a problem was brewing because there had been a clear hint of it in Mike's voice. But that was with hindsight. Even so, he should have grasped the reality of the threat and gone round to their offices immediately. He had always prided himself on being alert to the prospect of danger, but this time his sixth sense had failed. He wasn't used to that.

'Come on, sweetheart, it may look grim.' said Gill teasingly 'But you know it could be so much worse - one of these days you might become a stand up comedian.'

The sound of her voice with its unique resonance never failed; it was the surest and sweetest restorative of all. He perked up enough to give her a wan smile, accepting to himself that what had started out as a sequence of relatively harmless incidents, had gradually turned into something potentially more lethal.

'This affair looks more sinister.' His voice had tailed off, fishing around for the right choice of words 'I wouldn't mind betting it was our wretched picture he was looking for. But why? How can a landscape be so important?' He wasn't being dismissive, just hoping an answer would somehow pop up out of the blue.

'Well,' said Gill in her matter of fact way 'it's obvious that it must be the picture they are after. But it would help if we knew *why*, wouldn't it?

Gill, as always, managed to spot the blindingly obvious. And Ben knew she was right. They had to know why. Other than by learning more from the painting itself, who could possibly throw light on this bewildering business?

There were really only two people. Closest was Sue who, for obvious reasons, was turning into a bit of a mystery. Ben freely admitted to himself that he was more than a little intrigued by her, and it wasn't difficult to imagine that working more closely with her would have real advantages....but of course the last thing he needed right now were complications of that sort. More importantly there was her husband; an unknown quantity, vaguely connected to the Parnassos region, what was he up to?

The only other person was Androustes. What did Ben make of him? Recalling the notion that all men were rogues, Ben thought that Leonides might just be one, and being a Greek the odds probably higher. Why, for instance, hadn't George left Leonides the painting? The answer might be quite simply be because he was miles away in Athens. Leonides was a man who clearly believed that family was important, so his loyalties certainly lay with his cousin, George.

But Androustes *was* a Greek. And as far as Ben was concerned, that meant he was probably no more trustworthy than a hungry dog in a kitchen. Yet the more he thought about it, the more his instinct strengthened in favour of Androustes. With obvious caution, he concluded that the best option would be to choose Leonides. There would be fewer complications and he liked him. A visit to Athens might bring things to a head.

14.

Gill's phone rang. Reaching for it, it went dead almost immediately. Odd, she thought, particularly since it wasn't quite seven in the morning. A second later it started to ring again. This time Ben grabbed it.

'Hullo!' he said in a commanding voice 'Hang on,' searching for a shirt, a duvet, anything he could lay his hands on for warmth and decency, he got back on the phone 'sorry about that…who's that?'

'It's Cedric. I hope I'm not disturbing the peace.' His voice was tentative, if not properly confused. Catching his breath, he went on 'Giles gave me your number. He gave me Gill's too, but she wasn't there.'

'Yes, Cedric, it's me, I'm here;' he said reassuringly 'its me, Ben. But it's Gill's phone.'

'Oh, I see.' said Cedric, even though he didn't. 'I was doing some more cleaning yesterday, focussing on the area of the sheds, round where the little white cross stands. Christians tend to think all bits of joined up stick are some sort of cross. Anyway, it started me thinking along other lines, a cross-staff for example.'

Cedric was in full flow. Apparently he had been ruminating about the early days of navigation when sailors found out where they were by measuring the height of the sun at noon. It also turned them blind, he said. When they were within sight of land they also took what they called 'horizontal' angles to calculate their distance off the coast. He had now concluded that what we had all thought was a cross, might turn out to be a cross-staff.

True, after still more thought, he saw that it couldn't be a cross-staff, nor an astrolabe. Nothing like that, it wasn't nautical

61

at all. The small white thing looked more like a *dioptra,* a surveying instrument used by the ancient Greeks. So accurate was it, so far ahead of its time as a surveying instrument, that the ancient Greeks used it to build impressive aqueducts, like the one at Eupalinian. They also used a *dioptra* to tunnel with cunning accuracy through hills from both ends simultaneously, as they had done on the island of Samos. Cedric had been hard at work telephoning all and sundry; and, having checked out the possibility that it might be a *dioptra*, he was now exalted, his spirits soaring like a bird in flight. The thing is, he shouted down the telephone, this was an instrument that could be used to measure distance! The restorer of pictures could hardly contain himself; he fancied he might be on the brink of discovering how the painting might be communicating its message. He was convinced it showed you where to search for things, not only by direction, but also – and this was key – by distance. He had no idea what sort of things had been hidden so long ago. In his opinion, what most people tended to bury was treasure, and he sounded really pleased with that prospect.

Cedric wanted to show Ben how a *dioptra* could measure distance. Would he come round as soon as he could?

Ben told Cedric he would be round in about an hour and rang off. Turning to Gill, he asked if she would like to come? She didn't hesitate.

'Get yourself looking respectable', he said 'and we'll celebrate with a Full English somewhere on the way.

She was so pleased to see Ben quickly becoming his old self again. In her book, there was nothing like action being the cure for most people's problems.

ooooo

On the way to South Kensington, Gill, who was driving Ben's car, nearly had an accident. It wasn't her fault. She had had to brake quickly at the lights, which many other Londoners wouldn't have thought necessary, and the man behind her nearly drove into the back of their car. Soon after they stopped at an impressively up-market hotel for breakfast. It was only when they were once again motoring along that she happened to notice that the car behind them was the self-same car that had nearly bumped into them earlier on.

'Either he's following us,' said Gill 'or he just wants to dent your car.'

'Let's turn in somewhere. Here, coming up, now.' he said sharply. 'On your left.' Ben's incisive tone showed how quickly he had grasped the urgency of the situation.

By pulling in to the narrow forecourt of a small office block the car behind had no alternative but to continue. Turning in his seat to get a better view of the driver as he went past, Ben imagined he might have seen him before. Oh, no, not him! Ben suddenly realized who it was. Could he have been tailing them to find out where they kept the picture?

They soon reached Giles's studio. Sifonia wasn't there, but Giles's portrait was. In what, by now, had become very much his corner, Cedric was flourishing a piece of string, a protractor and a length of measuring tape. Bemused, he looked like a man who thought he had won the lottery, but had mislaid the ticket.

'What's up,?' said Ben greeting him warmly, having introduced Gill.

'Some and some' replied Cedric ambiguously. 'I've been tinkering with the painting. With not much luck. No sight of land this tide, I'm afraid.'

'I don't quite follow' Ben cut in, before getting completely lost.

63

'You see this?' Cedric was pointing at the small white object '
I'm pretty sure it's not a cross. I think it's a *dioptra*. Here, take
a closer look' he said, handing Ben a large magnifying glass.

Sure enough what Ben saw could, to a casual observer, be a cross;
but it had something that looked a bit like a saucer, a sort of circle
across the top, something disc-shaped. Straightening up he said 'I
think I see what you mean.'

'It really could be a *dioptra*' said Cedric hoping that with more
emphasis on the word it might turn out to be so.

'My dear Cedric, yesterday you were sure it was a cross!'

'I know, I know. But like the rest of natures struggling bipeds,
picture restorers can sometimes be wrong. I was probably
having a religious hallucination; one does you know, it's as a
result of cleaning so many old masters; you will be aware many
have a religious theme. Anyway, the point is that *dioptras* are
a sort of sighting tube, a rod with sights at both ends, attached
to a stand – very like this thing. If fitted with protractors they
could measure angles so it could be used for triangulation.
Euclid had one.' Cedric thought this last point was a clincher.
'This simple measuring device was the forerunner of the
theodolite. I believe it is telling us where to look.'

'It begs the question of how far along the dotted line.'

'Precisely! That's what's giving me a headache.'

Ben had an idea. Reaching for his wallet he pulled out what
looked like a yellowing cigarette paper. Glancing at it he turned to
Cedric saying

'Do you know anything about the Greek letter *phi*? Does it

mean anything to you?'

'Well, to be accurate, yes followed by no. Should it? You mean *phi*, as in fee, phi, pho, phumb? If I'm not wrong it comes somewhere towards the end of the Greek alphabet – somewhere after upsilon' Cedric, always a fund of arcane knowledge, could sometimes be unexpectedly accurate. He then went on to say that it meant absolutely nothing to him.

Ben pondered other possible connections, concentrating on finding a numerical connection. But he drew a blank. Once more he felt a pressing need to be able to consult a Greek, and resolved to contact Leonides. As though reading his thoughts, Cedric came up with the suggestion that someone ought to go to Greece; for in his opinion some surveying in the region of Parnassos was urgently required. In a matter of seconds the idea took hold that both of them should make an expedition to Parnassus. Ben told Cedric that his diary was going to be free quite soon. What would suit him?

'Not too soon.' said Cedric, his voice tinged with obvious disappointment. 'I could join you a little later. I've been neglecting work that's urgently required for an exhibition at the Maritime Museum, and I absolutely can't let them down. At the outside it will take about ten days, so I should be able to join you any time after that.'

'On reflection, that might work even better. I've plenty to deal with here. And there are people in Athens I would like to see, which would take a couple of days. When you come out, I'll meet you at the airport in a car and we can go straight on to Parnassos. The man I particularly want to see is Leonides Androustes, a cousin of George – you know, the man who left us the painting.

Ben and Gill had to be getting back, so he made a date to talk to Cedric within the next couple of days to finalise their arrangements. Before leaving, Ben asked Giles if he could keep their painting somewhere out of harm's way in his studio, if possible out of sight. Giles agreed to a place that Ben had spotted earlier among a rack of canvasses stacked on their side. The nearly cleaned painting was now quite dry so no harm would come to it.

Driving back, he and Gill excitedly ran through the benefits of a Greece visit. But the first question was how to get hold of Leonides. Not by asking Sue, who would obviously know. Then Ben had a flash of inspiration. In his notebook, a small book with an elastic band on the back to keep it closed, he had kept a record of the people he had met with George in Athens, all of them of course being *fogs*. Unless he was mistaken, he would find Androustes's details there. Ben felt elated at the prospect of seeing George's cousin again.

A map of the Parnassus region was something he badly needed. It had to be on a reasonably large scale, and in sufficient detail to give him the lie of the land.

15

Ben finally got through to Leonides in Athens. His response was immediate and welcoming. In his view the ancient tradition of Greek hospitality – Leonides referred to it by the word *proxenos* – laid an obligation on a host, almost a sacred trust, to attend to every need his guest might have. Androustes made it clear to Ben that this was a tradition he would consider it an honour to live up to, and Ben could stay with him for as long as he liked. Naturally, Leonides wanted to know if there was anything he could do to help; all Ben had to do was to ask. Thinking quickly, Ben explained that his first port of call would probably be the British School in Athens, where he could check the history of some long forgotten episode. He would tell him later about the other things he might like to do.

Seconds after agreeing a date for him to arrive in Athens, there was a distinct 'click' and the line went completely dead. No matter what Ben did to his telephone, including redialling Androustes twice, he could get no response. So he called Gill, who answered immediately, assuring Ben that it wasn't his phone. As well as feeling frustrated, he was concerned. What else could he do? Ring Sue Karamanlis? Hardly. He would just have to wait for Leonides to call him back.

The following day Ben got the call, and Leonides quickly got to the point. He said his telephone was obviously being tapped, tapped by people so incompetent that in the end they had succeeded only in cutting the line off completely. He could guess who was behind such a fiasco and would get onto them immediately. Leonides then went on to say that he would like him to meet an old friend of his who could explain the background to this sort of behaviour. Ben said he was looking forward to seeing him a week on Tuesday.

oooooo

Ben needed to take with him to Greece a copy of the painting, if possible of about the same size. The painting had been photographed in its original state and twice during the process of removing Abbott's elaborate over-painting. What he needed was a reasonably high-resolution copy of how it looked now.

His best bet was an architect's office. Most big practices had one of those specially designed large machines for copying large plans and drawings. He hadn't seen her for quite a while, but Ben didn't hesitate to call his old friend, Camilla. She had read architecture at St Andrews, and through a mixture of charm and good looks, but mostly because she had an exceptional talent, her career had taken off. She had teamed up with another architect, later to become her husband, and together they created one of those success stories that had become a byword in the architectural profession. On the telephone the receptionist told Ben that Camilla was in Sweden. So he asked for David, Camilla's husband and partner in the practice.

'Of course I remember you, Ben!' Was he just being polite? No, Ben recalled that David probably had reason enough to remember him. 'Cam's away in Sweden being briefed for an extension to the museum in Upsala. She'll be back next week. Can I help?'

'I hesitate to ask, because it's a favour' he paused, but having got this far he continued 'I need to copy a painting, it's about 30 inches by 24 inches. I think that's about 75 by 60 centimetres....'

'Ben Benbow, I happen to know what an inch looks like...'

'Of course, of course! I was hoping you might be able to make a copy for me. I go to Athens next week and need to take it with me. Could you manage it?'

68

'Sure.' replied David, wondering what Ben was up to. 'Bring it round as soon as you like. You know where we are? Ask for Fiona: she'll sort it for you.'

Ben had now to get a move on, as he had to pick up the painting before running it round to David's office somewhere off the Albert Bridge Road on the embankment. There would just be time for a quick lunch with Cedric if he was free. He rang him, soon to hear the unmistakable booming of his recorded message:

"Ahoy! The restorer is adrift on a moonless sea, back soon, leave a ….."

interrupted by Cedric himself saying 'hang on I'm here, but I don't know how to stop this bloody machine.' There was a muffled crash at his end as he grappled with the recorder and dropped the receiver.

'Hullo, hullo. Who's that?'

'It's Ben. Have you any plans for lunch?'

'None. Why?'

'Let's meet. Can you make it to the Bombay Brasserie, just off the Gloucester Road, near the tube station. Say one o'clock – later if you like.'

'No, that's fine. See you then.'

oooooo

According to Ben's uncle, there were two things you needed to know about an Indian restaurant before deciding to eat there. The first was to be sure that the restaurant was in fact Indian and not Bangladeshi; the second was to know if their popadams were any

69

good. Ben knew that at the Brasserie there was never any doubt.

Cedric and Ben settled for the menu of the day – a mild, anglicised curry with basmati rice.

'Cedric, I go to Athens a week on Tuesday' he said, following an approving crunch. 'When will you be able to follow?'

'A bit later, I'm afraid. I have to see what sort of progress I can make with one of the paintings I'm cleaning. The trouble is, it's huge: you may not know it but Stanfield started his career as scenery painter at Drury Lane. So his sense of scale often can run away with him. It's only a light clean. I'll know better in a day or two.'

He enjoyed working on Clarkson Stanfield's colourful, often dramatic compositions: Stanfield had a knack of being able to draw you in towards the focal point of the activity. Though a contemporary of Turner, he had never, ever seen himself – even with one of his very best seascapes – as in any sense a rival. But then no-one did.

Ben judged this was the right moment to get Cedric interested in an idea that had been occupying a lot of his time recently, the many mysteries of *Phi*.

'You know I found a piece of paper in a groove of the frame?' Cedric did remember and nodded, sipping his coffee. 'The only thing written on it was the Greek letter Φ. Well I've been talking to a friend, an addict of quirky maths, and he spent ages talking me through the intricacies of *Phi*. Apparently it's known as a Golden Number, though in fact it's just a ratio. First discovered by a Greek sculptor and architect called Phidias – hence *Phi* – it has been credited with wide ranging influence over the last two thousand years'.

Maths was not a subject close to Cedric's heart and this became obvious as his eyelids began to droop, a signal that he was off on one of his longer sea voyages. A sharp cough from Ben brought Cedric back to a state of nearly full attention.

Ben explained that Phi was a ratio between lengths, one being Φ times longer than the other. It was used for the façades of temples, the Parthenon being a fine example; and it worked for artists too, the ratio between the length and width of a face. Leonardo de Vinci used it in his illustrations for *De Divina Proportione.* Ben thought that was enough.

> 'So you see, Cedric, it has been around a long time. Widely accepted in Ancient Greece as a number with almost mystical properties, it was a touchstone for perfection.' Then he added 'You might care to know that the actual ratio is **1: 1.6180339887.**'

Quoting the number from the notepad in his wallet, Ben's voice grew markedly louder, as if he had just put on a pair of headphones. The couple at the next-door table stopped talking, turning to stare at him in awe or, possibly, fear.

Cedric was not a good listener and thankful that Ben had finally furled his sails. He had listened to enough to understand that Ben's ratio was about one and a half to one, and started trawling through his memory for any details of the painting that might answer, bringing to mind any length or feature that might – in the same ratio – also give them a distance. He could find no obvious connection.

> 'You said you were about to make a copy of our painting to take to Greece.'

The '*our*' implied that Cedric had assumed some sort of joint ownership, which Tom welcomed. Not only was it a sign that Cedric was fully on board for their journey of discovery, the 'our' also pointed to the fact that it had become a joint venture. Cedric had great descriptive powers, which enlivened the time they spent together and Ben naturally warmed to him. He found his imagined sailor's vocabulary amusing and enjoyed his endless stories. Sometimes he couldn't help but notice, even though they were much the same age, that Cedric's foibles tended to be those of a rather older man, at least a man from a bygone age, probably about a hundred and eighty years old. Ben put it down to Cedric's lonely life as a restorer, and guessed he was probably in his early thirties.

'Yes, that would work well. Let's both go round to Giles after we've finished here.'
They got into Ben's car and headed towards South Kensington. On the way Cedric began to mull over what Ben had said about Phi. The first measurement he ought to make should be of the frame itself. If he were a betting man, which he wasn't, he would wager his whole collection of Henty novels that the ratio would be whatever Ben had said it was – one point six something to one. After that he would have to take another, closer look at the painting.

Soon they were outside the stuccoed front of the house in Waverley Gardens, and in a few seconds were climbing the stairs leading to Giles's studio. Sifonia opened the door. She looked radiant, every movement she made enhanced by the ripple of her mauve sarong. Not an easy colour to wear, thought Ben, but on her a sensation. Cedric, for his part, found himself wishing he had been a painter, not just a plain old restorer.

Giles, she said, wasn't at home. He had been summoned to contribute an opinion to a news programme scheduled to go out on TV that evening. He wouldn't be back for a couple of hours.

Ben quickly explained that all he wanted was the painting, so he went over to the rack of canvasses behind the cupboard and rummaged about until he found it. Finding the frame took longer, but it was there and they placed the stretched canvas loosely inside. Siphonia volunteered another of her sarongs, this one dark green, to wrap the parcel in and all too soon they were ready for the off – rather reluctantly it. They had learnt she was going home to Jakarta in a day or two for at least a couple of months to attend to family affairs.

From South Ken across the Kings Road and over the Albert Bridge it took them less than twenty minutes. In no time they were across the threshold and into the offices of Ablett Loftts. They asked for Fiona, who turned out to be a serious-looking twenty something year-old with a high forehead and little sense of humour. Explaining that she was Camilla's PA, she led them along a series of interlocking corridors with poise and efficiency until they reached a slightly less glamorous section of open-plan rooms. There, in the corner, stood a very modern but obviously capable machine. Thankfully Fiona knew exactly what to do, and within ten minutes had produced two faithful colour copies. After a pause to check their quality she rolled them up and pushed them into a cardboard cylinder. Handing it to Ben, with a searching look, she asked herself what it was that her boss might once upon a time have found so attractive in him. She wasn't sure, and with so little to go on she knew she would have to be guessing in the dark.

○○○○○○

Rather than taking the painting back to Giles's flat, Cedric suggested they take it back to his place in Greenwich, where they could both have a good look at it and see whether there was anything in Ben's theory about Φ. They headed down the Old Kent Road through Deptford towards the atmospheric cluster of buildings at the heart of old Greenwich. Cedric made a pot of coffee while Ben unwound Sifonia's green sarong from the painting. The first sign that Φ might be connected to their landscape was indeed the relationship of height to width; Cedric's measuring was fastidious and the width of the painting turned out to be precisely 1.6 times its height. His collection of Henty novels was safe.

But what could a ratio mean in the context of the picture? They gazed at it intently, willing it to shed some light. Did it relate in some way to the little white cross-like marker in the lower right section? Could it have anything to do with those buildings? The painting remained mute. Ratios were not making any sense. Phi must have some other connotation.

After a few minutes Ben, declining Cedric's offer of a drink, said he would head home to Gill. Leaving the painting with Cedric, he made the journey back up the Old Kent Road.

oooooo

By the time he made it home, Gill was already there. For all her breezy self-confidence, she seemed a bit muted, more vulnerable than usual. The colour of her dark hair, catching and reflecting the light behind her as she moved her head, shone with occasional flashes of blue. Ben gave her a long, comforting hug, feeling a surge of anticipation, of longing.

'Cedric sends his love' he said.

'Where have you been?'

'We, Cedric and I, picked up the painting from Giles's studio to have it copied, they're in this cardboard tube and I'll show you in a second. He and I have been trying to see how the *phi* ratio might fit in. We don't think it does.'

He had slipped his hand round her back as he talked and pulled her gently to him. She pressed her body against his kissing him noiselessly in the ear. Ben felt his concentration slipping but managed to keep some sort of focus on recent events.

'It's a peculiar thing but just recently I've been feeling unexpectedly close to poor old George, to the extent that I can almost feel his presence. In a sense it was George that urged me to put *phi* to one side and go out to Athens. I felt I had to get on with it.'

'What do you expect to find?'

'I really don't know. Maybe buried treasure, who knows? A quantity of old gold would certainly make the trip worthwhile …'

'Not in Athens surely?'

' No. The place to investigate is the mountain. That means I'll have to climb Parnassos, perhaps a trek over the top to Delphi.' He was smiling mischievously.

'Be careful, Ben darling. Remember curiosity killed the cat. And you know that curiosity is a very serious weakness of yours. You're quite capable of judging just how far to go, but you can't resist going that little bit further, can you?' Her touch was light, but she was serious. What was giving her cause for alarm was Ben's untameable curiosity

But now wasn't the moment to have doubts, to let little eddies of worry rustle about in the backwater of her mind. A bottle of Paternina's *Banda Azul* stood on the top of the bookcase and two steaks were quietly marinating in a concoction of hers that had Moroccan origins.

16.

In the few minutes before his plane touched down, Ben peered through the prism of his window at the world below, feasting his eyes on the wide variety of inevitable blue. All around was the triumphant blue of a cloudless sky and, below, the darker hue of sea - fringed with white where the Saronic Gulf lapped the shores of Attica. Further south he could just make out the first of the Cyclades, like diamonds sparkling on the cobalt surface of the Aegean. Filled with intense anticipation, a line from Shelley, *we are all Greeks now*, drifted through his consciousness.

Throwing his case onto the back seat of a hired car and placing the cardboard tube alongside it with rather more care, he headed north to the city. The first problem he was going to have to address was how to deal with the enquiries that Leonides was bound to heap on him the minute he arrived. How much should he trust him?

That problem soon appeared insignificant compared with the mindless battle being waged on the road to central Athens from the airport. In stark contrast to the famously irresistible charm of the Greeks, the users of the road appeared to hate each other with such deep animosity that they wished each other dead.

Bearing in mind that his objective was to explore Mount Parnassos, Ben didn't much relish the prospect of getting stuck in Athens for any length of time. Of course there was always the majesty of the Parthenon perched above the city on the Acropolis, and many other wonderful relics of a glorious past. But the city itself lay in something of a bowl, surrounded by hills and escarpments, making it unbearably hot and windless in the summer months and desolate in winter. Few redeeming features were to be found in the general architecture of the city itself, a legacy of the destructive war with Turkey in 1923 and the vandalism rampant during the short epoch under the Colonels, when any pretence at planning permission had been dispensed with. What you tended to see now were slab-sided '60s structures each beginning to show their age, and dreadfully crowded streets wherever you went. For the few days that Ben planned to be in Athens he could easily put up with it.

oooooo

Leonides lived in a house that had belonged to his family for generations, almost since the Ottoman Turks had rolled up their carpets and departed for home. Only parts of the rambling old building dated from those early days, the rooms furthest from the street with their higher ceilings, which dated from the end of the eighteenth century; the rest had been rebuilt about fifty years ago. His house was off Lazarietou Square, with the main entrance from Tzami Karatasi.

Late in the afternoon, having found a space to park his car, he stood in front of what turned out to be a modern entrance door. To the right were three buzzers and instinct told him to go for the bottom one. He gave it a push. Nothing happened for a while and he was about to go for the next button when the door started to open, very slowly. Noiselessly, it turned on its hinges, revealing a slightly bent old lady, her grey hair in a neat bun on top of her head. Despite her stoop she retained an air of elegance. She appeared surprised to see him, but when he gave his name her serious face broke into a welcoming smile. She opened the door fully and waved him in. From what he could understand, she seemed to be saying that Mr Androustes was out and would be back between five and six; she tried to make this clear by pointing with the appropriate number of fingers at the clock in the hall.

Ben already knew that Leonides was going be out that afternoon. He picked up his case from where he had dumped it by the front door, and followed the old lady up to his room. Using gestures like a traffic policeman, he endeavoured to convey to her that he

77

was happy to wait downstairs. So she stayed on the landing before taking him down again into what he guessed must be the drawing room.

A comfortable, long room with windows running down one side, it tuned into an 'L' shape at the far end where Ben noticed an ornate piano. Despite being a sizeable room it had so much furniture, so much general bric-a-brac, there was little real sense of space; in fact, thought Ben, if you had a cat this would hardly be an ideal place to swing it. He prowled about for a minute or two, gazing in wonder at the hoard of memorabilia perched wherever there was space, before settling down on the sofa with a magazine.

Drinking in the atmosphere, both the strangeness of it all and the evidence everywhere of Greece's easily identifiable culture, he was enraptured by his surroundings. Ben was one of those people who felt completely at ease abroad, possibly because he had been brought up 'abroad' in Trinidad. That was before spending his school and university years in England where, if he was honest, he had never felt he quite fitted in, if only because he wasn't a completely home-bred native; there remained in him a trace of something slightly, yet stubbornly foreign. Some of the girls he had known might have preferred to say of him that they found him slightly exotic, sometimes a useful attribute. Coming from the 'wrong box', he found it easy to think and look outside it.
And compared to those who were genuinely native to the British Isles, who tended to have a quite insular view of abroad, he found it relatively easy to understand foreigners and their culture, feeling instantly at home wherever he was abroad. 'Where you are, is your country' was a sentiment that very much applied to Ben and he felt this to be the case even in Athens; and that was without speaking a word of the language. He had much to thank his childhood in Trinidad for, but it did make him wonder just how Cedric was going to be able to cope.

Before very long there was activity in the hall and the imposing figure of Leonides Androutses strode in, larger than life.

' *Kolypson ikos*!' bellowed his host, knowing full well that Ben didn't speak a word of Greek. 'Welcome home! You my *proxenos'* he emphasised the word, 'my house is your house. Safe journey?'

'Fine, thanks. Good of you to have me to stay. Your house is lovely.'

'Pleased you like it. Tonight dinner an old friend comes, Alex Metaxa. I hope you find him interesting. H'e professor he say of modern history, that is our history starting about 1820. Don't be deceived by your school teaching, Greece is a modern country.'

Greeks when speaking English often experience difficulty in the way they pronounce their 'h's, having a tendency to rip off an unexpected dottle with their 'h's. Leonides was no exception but otherwise he had a fine grasp of the English vocabulary.

'Alex is bringing h'is daughter, Melina, who is in love with me.' Looking at Ben he morphed his face into a monstrous wink. 'It is her father who'll give you the background you seek, Melina will make the evening tolerable to me.'

Leonides was in a good mood, partly due to Ben's arrival , but mostly it seemed at the prospect of being with a pretty girl at supper. Other things were on his mind, though, for he had noticed Ben's tube, which he had left in the hall.

'You have brought it with you, the painting?'

'A copy.'

79

'That'll do. Shall we look at it – we see it in my room?'
It was a question that didn't need an answer, as Leonides had
started moving towards the door. Ben picked up the tube and
followed him along the corridor to his study, clearly a very private
room for he had to unlock it. He motioned Ben in and started
clearing an area on the wide mahogany work surface by the
window. Leonides was one of those men who preferred to stand at
a desk.

His study was a less spacious room with a single sash window
at the far end from the door. The walls on either side were lined
with book shelves, not all of them holding books. Spaces had been
created to house the sort of personal treasures that men all over
the world tend to collect. There was a half-hull model of a dark
blue patrol boat with '*aktophulaki*' painted in yellow on the side,
which, judging by the quasi-military stripes, Ben took to mean
Coastguard. Not far along from that was a pair of muzzle-loading
18th century pistols with fine, inlaid tracery of gold leaf on their
dull metal barrels. In pride of place on the middle of the shelf,
was a marble head. In profile and lit by a small beam of light from
overhead, it was evidently from antiquity and Ben guessed it must
be Apollo. On the shelves opposite was an old print showing the
dispositions of the Athenian and Persian fleets at the battle of
Salamis and next to it, an engraved chart of Ithaca. This one was
beautifully embellished with scrolls and wind icons in the style of
the ancient *anemoi.* The whole room, punctuated by random piles
of books stacked vertically on the floor, spoke eloquently of its
owner and his interests.

Ben started unpicking the tape from around the end of the cylinder
and soon he was able to let the rolled up photo slide out of the
tube. He held it gently as he untied the ribbon holding it in a roll.

'It's a photograph' he said guardedly, though that much would
soon be obvious. Ben remembered that Leonides had last seen

the canvas in Gill's flat before any restoration work had been started. 'But it's in high definition, as you will see. Here, take a look.'

Winding the copy in the reverse direction to make it lie flat, he laid it on the table. It was a good copy. At first glance you might even have thought that it was the real thing had it not been for the slightly glossy finish. Leonides was as eager as a terrier.

'Good God!' was all he said, in low measured tones. 'It is *the* painting all right, and it's more or less what I had hoped.' Staring in disbelief, he bent over it to get a closer look at the detail, his head no more than 18 inches from the table.

Breathing heavily with excitement, he managed to wheeze out just one more word, 'Fantastic!' he said. Then turning towards Ben, he continued

'You no understand what this is,' tapping the photograph lightly with his cigarette holder. 'No-one,' he paused to emphasise his meaning, 'no-one to know about it. You tell no-one.'

He turned to Ben saying they had much to talk about. Leading the way back to the drawing room, he asked his housekeeper as they passed her in the hall to bring them a tray of tea. Ben noticed that Leoniides had carefully re-locked his study door.

She brought in the tray of tea, with a plate of small pastries, appearing to linger as she placed the tray between them. As she left, Leonides said rather formally that they did not wish to be disturbed, a remark that could only have been directed at her as there was no-one else in the house. They sat facing each other in silence, sipping their tea. After a brief interval Leonides seemed to start fretting about something – he even produced his κομνολοι – his worry beads. Made of a very light metal, they had a distinctive light sound when being clicked round on their thread.

'What you have there,' as he spoke he gestured down the corridor 'is a copy of what must be one of our most sought after paintings: it is the key to an old mystery.'

Leonides, apart from excitement, allowed a note of pride to creep into his voice as he described the circumstances surrounding the life of his ancestor. Apparently, rumours of the existence of a painting had been circulating for ages, for it was thought to show where his ancestor, Odysseus, had hidden his horde of gold and the many statues and icons that he had looted. The gold, was real enough, it had been shipped from London to fund Greece's war of liberation. Conveyed in an English frigate to Zakinthos in the Ionian, it had then to be forwarded to Byron in Missolonghi to enable him to purchase arms and train soldiers. But as, Ben would learn later, Byron died before this could be effected.

Leonides added that the gold was known to be *in specie,* in coins.

'Mostly English sovereigns but Hollander dollars as well, which were also in circulation at the time. All was gold.'

Leonides's black eyes were burning brightly as he trawled the recesses of his memory.

'In his cave – the one in the painting – Odysseus used old tin boxes to keep his bullion in,' he stretched his arms wide indicating their length 'tins that once had contained English gun-powder.'

Many guns, and of course powder, had been brought up to the cave from Missolonghi by a young Englishman, an artillery officer called Whitmore. Ben remembered only a little about the Greek War of Liberation from his school days. Byron had been appointed by the London Greek Committee to manage their affairs in strife torn Greece. Arriving in Zakinthos from Italy he had sailed over to Missolonghi, choosing to base himself there and make the place his headquarters. Missolonghi, virtually a swamp, was known to be an unhealthy area, and for Byron it proved a death trap. There, in 1824, he died. No obvious successor was to hand.

'Look,' said Leonides, pausing to look at his watch 'we come back this later. You go your room, for shower; then we start serious business of the evening.'

Ben welcomed the suggestion. He went up to his room, leaving Leonides in the drawing room, or so he had thought, but as soon he was on the stairs he noticed that Leonides was heading back to his study, where the copy of the painting lay.

○○○○○○

By eight o'clock Ben, refreshed and thirsty, found his way downstairs and along the corridor to the drawing room. There he caught sight of Leonides talking intently to another man. On hearing Ben's approach, their conversation ended and Leonides waved Ben forward to introduce him to Alexis Metaxa with a flourish of both hands. Their friendship had clearly been cemented by years of familiarity, and Ben got the impression that Alexis had been well briefed by his friend.

For a man his age, Metaxa had boyish good looks. His black hair, with just a few wisps of grey, had been trimmed short. Small and energetic, he wore a loose, blue cotton jacket over a crumpled blue shirt. He looked comfortable and relaxed. Being an academic and a lively sort of man, he had a tendency to use rapid jabbing movements of his forefinger to emphasise what he was saying. Ben could easily see him holding the attention of a crowded lecture hall.

83

'Alexis' Metaxa said 'but everyone calls me Alex.' He spoke very good English and, unlike Androustes, with only with a moderate accent. 'I've heard a lot about you from Leo' he said, pointing in the direction of his friend, who was standing at a table with bottles and glasses on it, pouring a drink for Ben.

Ben had felt nervous asking for a gin and tonic. Some years earlier he had bought a bottle labelled *London Dry Gin* from a store on one of the Greek islands, and when he added ice and tonic, the drink had turned completely opaque, reminiscent more of *ouzou*. Leonides had a triumphant look on his face as he came towards them, suggesting complete confidence in the drink.

' Thanks,' said Ben, adding 'Cheers! I'm afraid my Greek isn't up to much.'

'Youssou!' they announced in chorus, with Alex adding 'No problem.'

Ben noticed that a table had been laid outside in the courtyard adjoining the drawing room. It had been laid for four people. Where was his daughter? As if reading his thoughts, Alex explained that Melina was going to be late and would be joining them before long.

'So what do you want to know about our Revolution?' said Alex.

'I would like to know about the Klephtic bands, the warlords that terrorised the countryside in the 1820's.'

'It depends what you mean by Klepht. There were quite a few of these groups, which in reality were more like tribes. Leonides should know, his ancestor was one of the most prominent. Your great, great, grandfather wasn't it?'

'Yes, was called Odysseus Androustes.' Said Leonides rolling off the famous name. 'Please one more 'great' Alex, I think. A hero. Our family come from Ithaca – giving his name Odysseus. But he grew up in Moldavia, a region of mountains in the north west, that no can sustain a buzzard or live a farmer and his children. Scrub and mountains, nothing to eat! Tough school, very good for boys who will be brigands.'

According to Alex, the Klephts were more than mere brigands. Although it was the Orthodox Church that played a key role in keeping alive the Hellenic *geist*, the Klephts also contributed in a major way.

'What everyone has forgotten,' Alex meant except the Greeks 'is that the Ottoman Turks ruled Greece for nearly 400 years. So long under the Turks, the Greeks were in danger of forgetting who they were. Then, in 1814, three men – part of the widespread *diaspora* in the earlier eighteenth century – met in Odessa and formed a movement that became known as the *Philiki Eteria.*'

Alex talked more about the brigands and the influence of the Philiki. He was an excellent tutor and time slipped by.

Well into dinner – grilled lamb on a bed of couscous – they had got as far as their second bottle of *retsina*. Ben, fearing that this might still be one bottle short of when it became drinkable, showed a great deal of restraint. Just then, there was a bustle in the hall and Melina swept in. She kissed her father, but made a greater fuss over Leonides, who responded with evident delight.

'Ben Benbow' he said, looking deeply into her eyes. She shook Ben's hand and placed herself next to him, nodding to the offer of a glass of wine as she did so.

Melina had none of her father's looks. A pleasant open face and shoulder length blonde hair – more honey coloured than blonde – she was in her late twenties. While not being what most people would instantly recognise as pretty, she was good looking, and her face had fine features. But her whole persona took off the minute she opened her mouth, for she had a deep, deep voice, a growl that suggested at least 40 cigarettes a day, even though she had never smoked. Her voice spoke from her very soul. Ben was fascinated. There was no more talk of Klepths, and the conversation turned to Melina's early evening, which had been a final rehearsal for a concert on the following evening – she played the cello in an orchestra of mostly young musicians. Leonides was putty in her hands, responding to each sentence she uttered with delight. He was boyishly pleased with the way everything was going.

The evening lasted well beyond midnight until first Melina, then her father, took their leave. As she was saying goodnight, Melina leant across to Tom and said she would call him in the morning.

oooooo

As good as her word, the phone rang after 9 o'clock. The house keeper handed Ben the receiver with a knowing smile. Leonides had already gone out, leaving instructions that breakfast for Tom should be a huge quantity of bacon and eggs. In fact, all he wanted was a cup of coffee.

'Hi' he said 'you got home …'

'Yes. Look, how's this for an idea?'

Oh, that voice! How did she get such a chronically suggestive kind of voice? She must have been a singer in a smoke filled nightclub when she was a teenager.

'Would you like to get out of Athens? I thought you might enjoy a trip to a spectacular old fortress overlooking the Gulf of Corinth. I know you've only just arrived, so how about the weekend – what about Saturday? We could spend the night at a friend's house near there.'

'Sounds great' said Ben, hoping she would go on talking for ever.

She told Ben that her father also wanted to have a word with him and, giving him Alex's number, she was gone. A few minutes later he was through to Alex, who suggested they meet at his usual taverna at noon. The timing suited him well as he could spend the afternoon round in the Souidias visiting the British School. With any luck he would be able to have a good chat with the very bright girl who ran it. He would ring first to warn her that he was seeking all the information she could lay her hands on relating to the *Philiki Eteria.*

oooooo

Alex was sitting behind a lattice screen on the left of the entrance at the rather shabby taverna known as the *Actiom*. It was nearly empty as it was still much too early for lunch. Alex was in fine form, bubbling away about the politics of the city, and wondering about the wisdom of an investment mooted by a friend only that morning in a manufacturing company somewhere in the vicinity of Marathon.

He quickly turned to the subject that interested Ben – what had become of the *Philiki Eteria* since the early, revolutionary days of the 1820's? Apparently it still existed though it had devolved and split into two factions, two distinct brotherhoods that had kept going over the years by evolving into associations more appropriate to the times. The proper inheritor of the old brotherhood was still the *Philiki Eteria* of earlier days. As before,

87

they continued to focus on the spirit of things Greek, to safeguard the legacy of ancient Greece and to preserve the timeless identity of Hellas. They were strongly opposed to ancient artefacts being sold abroad or finding their way onto the global market, pursuing the dream one day of returning to Greece all her missing treasures, including the Elgin marbles at the the British Museum, the Venus de Milo at the Louvre and all the bits and pieces that litter the shelves of museums around the world. This, the real *Philiki,* had noble aims and retained the vision of its founders. However, the other division, known colloquially as the *ana-philiki*, had mutated to a very different kind of order. They, too, were concerned with things that had to do with Greece, but they were in it for gain. These people more resembled a sort of *mafioso* and if they could make a turn by selling old artefacts that was fine. With a few refinements they had mostly retained the bandit characteristics of their ancestors, stealing or physically looting anything they could get hold of that had value. They could also be vicious.

Alex told Ben that many old Greek families had strings linking them to the turmoil of the past. Leonides was a fine example as his ancestor had been a warlord ruling over the Boeticean plain with ruthless force. Sadly, old Odysseus had come to a sticky end. Before his death though, the old man was thought to have buried a vast amount of loot, much of which he had plundered from churches and other historical sites in the Peleponesse. And naturally there was also much talk of gold bullion.

Alex hoped this background would be helpful, but there was something else he wanted to touch on as he had noticed Ben's reaction to Melina at the dinner table.

'In Greece' said Alex 'the past is always with us; everyone carries the weight of some sort of event linking them and their lives to the past.'

Ben grasped what he meant. While it wasn't always easy to put your finger on it, there were moments in some of the older countries like Greece when the past knocked on many front doors, the past becoming indistinguishable from the present. You could sense it almost subliminally, you knew very well that it was there.

'What you need to know, Ben, is that I am not Melina's real father. She knows, of course. Her father and I were boyhood friends on the island of Skiathos, where her father earned a living from sponge diving – a very unhealthy activity, as you may know. Sadly, he died in an accident at sea, drowning when his boat sank during a vicious *meltemi*, a boat that in most people's opinion should never have gone to sea. Melina was only five years old.'

Alex was reliving the tragedy, an episode from his early years, culminating in the death of his old friend. With an effort he continued.

'You should also know that Melina is not completely Greek, her mother was French. A talented water-colourist, she came to the island to paint. But she stayed on having fallen for my friend Draco. He wasn't just a diver, he was a very handsome guy - always getting into trouble with the girls. Anyway, what started as a casual affair ended with them falling deeply in love. They got married and were a happy couple. Then Melina was born, and it was only a few years later that tragedy struck – first her father was drowned. But worse was to come, for six months later her mother also died.'

There was clearly more to it than that, but Ben thought it was not the moment to prompt Alex for more detail than he was prepared to give.

'At the time of course it was a seismic tragedy for little Melina.

89

But, with some help from me, she stood her ground and got on with life – and she has made a great success of it. I took her to Athens and became her father, mostly for legal reasons. It wasn't a case of adoption, or anything like that. In Greece, because over the years we have suffered so much from one disaster or another, often not of our making I should add, we are able to invoke a simple clause in our legal code when it is beneficial to do so."

He had started to return to his less serious, more out-going self, and, with a wave of both arms in a wide arc, he finished with a clap of his hands, as if to say that the subject had been dealt with. It was also to summon another cup of coffee.

'Melina should tell you her own story. She will tell it better, and it is better that she should. You will have to ask her. By the way, a very strong-minded person, she can be quite wild!'

oooooo

The British School's library is on one side of what had once been a large garden, shaded by acacia trees. When he reached the sheltered courtyard he was ushered into the slightly cramped quarters behind the few book-filled rooms. There he was handed a copy of a short treatise on the formation of the *Philiki Eteria*, and the pretty archivist whispered nervously that at first glance the Philiki seemed to have rather too much in common with the Freemasons. She left him to it, sitting under one of the acacia trees.

It was absorbing reading. The most chilling snippet lay in a paragraph about the structure of the organisation: formed before the start of the War of Independence, the organisation was run by a sinister triumvirate known as the *Invisible Authority* (the archivist was being proved right!), three men who gave orders that were followed with unquestioning obedience. Good grief, Ben thought: the *Invisible Authority* makes the Freemasons seem more like the Women's Institute. There was more. When becoming a member of the *Philiki Eteria* you took an oath of allegiance that was unbreakable – the invisible men would see to that – and you then became known as a *philikoi*. Finally, and he nearly overlooked the last sentence, which was key as it mentioned that the *philikoi* often used the sign of the Greek letter Φ to identify themselves to other members of the brotherhood.

17.

On his return, the housekeeper told Ben there had been a call for him. Meester Credit, please call him back. Of course, he would right away. Remembering the earlier tapping episode, Tom had momentary doubts about using it but he went ahead and asked Lela if he could use the phone. She pointed to it, by the front door; and left him to get on with it.

'Cedric, its Ben.'

'Thanks for calling back. The lady at your end didn't seem to have 20:20 hearing, and it's possible her English is a bit rusty. Anyway, she appears to have given you my message, which is that I'm booked to fly out on Friday.'

'Brilliant! Give me your flight details and I'll pick you up at the airport.'

'Now for the bad news. I'm afraid Giles's studio was broken into – the place rummaged from top to bottom. Whoever it was, literally turned his studio upside down. It's as though it had been hit by a tsunami. Giles was distraught. Happily his portrait of Siphonia was safe. A proper shambles.'

'What were they looking for? Cash, valuables? One of his paintings perhaps? I wouldn't say no to the one of Siphonia, would you? Could they have been after *our* painting?'

'Who knows?. I've said nothing to Giles.'

'Cedric, I take it you still have the painting …'

'Of course I bloody well have! In fact, I might even have difficulty finding it myself, so tidy is my flat. You see, I've turned over a new leaf; the new motto for my apartment is a place for everything and a place for everything else. '

'Cedric, that sounds serious. Looking forward to seeing you on Friday. I, too, could have some news for you, but it can wait.'

In fact, Ben had been thinking wistfully of Melina at the very moment Cedric told him he was coming out on Friday. Maybe the fates were watching over him - he was, after all, in the right country for the fates.

oooooo

With only a few days to go before Cedric arrived, Ben didn't have much time. His priority needed to be a serious talk with Leonides to learn everything he knew about the painting, and was it true that it had a message? If it did, where was it? Ben must tell him that there were too many unknowns for him to waste more time guessing.

He also longed to hear from Melina herself. What had been the nature of the tragedy that had clouded her early life? Alex, as well as being a well-informed and useful contact, was obviously a sensitive man who cared deeply about Melina. He seemed to have none of that persistent lust for money, so prevalent among Greeks. Ironic, thought Ben, that the out-and-out pursuit of wealth endemic among the Greek people should end up by making Greece such a poor country. Or was it simply that the pursuit of wealth in the DNA of just a relative few could be the reason why poverty afflicted so many of the rest?

Leonides was his top priority. Not only was Ben staying with him, and therefore in daily contact, but also Leonides was the closest link to the man, his cousin, who had started the hare running in the first place. He needed from Leonides a tangible sign that he could really trust him. Greeks tended to be a disputatious lot, with

93

incomprehensible family feuds rattling down the centuries. In Ben's humble experience, many of them were unreliable, just as many of them had a rather shifty look.

With the imminent arrival of Cedric, the next step was naturally going to be an expedition to Mount Parnassos where, because they would be more exposed – certainly more visible – the risks they would be running would necessarily be higher; and by then, neither he nor Cedric would have any control at all over what risks they might face.

oooooo

The opportunity came sooner than Ben expected. Leonides had returned from his morning ride in the wooded area over the hills on the eastern side of the city. Riding once a week had been his habit ever since he could remember; for sitting on a horse gave him a lot of pleasure as well as allowing him time for thinking through the issues of the day. He was also under the impression that riding, like swimming, exercised nearly all the muscles in his body. It was a noble activity and it was good for you.

Leonides had of course noticed that Ben needed some guidance, so he had already decided that his next step must to be to tell him everything he knew about his ancestor and his devious ways. The old man had a bad reputation for double-dealing, making little distinction between friend and foe. In fact, if there was one thing about him that was consistent it was the way he frequently changed sides when there was the least shift in the wind. This fault in his character made Odysseus a difficult man to follow, to know. Part of the problem was that he really had become a proper legend, his famous name lending an authenticity to all his deeds. It increased his stature, and this meant that some of the stories of his exploits were likely to be apocryphal: the problem of course was where the truth lay hidden. Leonides even suspected that there may have been a simpler motive behind some of the stories - to spread disinformation about his ancestor's activities. As soon as he got home, Leonides suggested to Ben that they have a cup of coffee in the courtyard and piece together more of the background.

'I've been hoping you would say that– the painting has been the cause of too much of head scratching. It's in your study, I think?

'Yes, I'll fetch it.' Leonides began raising his voice to seek the whereabouts of Lela who, on hearing it, appeared discreetly from around the corner. Had she been listening? Ben wondered. 'Coffee, please Lela. And no interruptions.'

He walked away with a purpose in his stride and soon re-joined Ben in the courtyard with the tube under his arm.

Once more Ben unrolled the copy and laid it on top of the wrought iron table. They both gazed at it without saying a word. Finally, Leonides broke the silence.

'Buried treasure!' said Leonides. There was an edge of excitement in his voice.

18.

Leonides dived into his subject like a bird of prey.

'All start with painting. Vrysakis, you know? Greek painter of early nineteenth century, good with clothes, landscape and snow if any. And scenery.' he said, remembering the word just in time. 'H'e very careful and true detail. One masterpiece was north face of Mount Parnassos – now painting in Greek embassy in London.'

Ben cut in to say that he had seen it and had noticed the detail given to shrubs and rocks, and of course the Cave.

'Possible paint this one,' Leonides continued 'because detail is good. Or may be copy. As you see, buildings have been added to smaller picture, and good reason for that. As well as show the *Mauvre Troupe,*' his 'r's came over firmly and strongly 'what show is where Odysseus treasure hidden. How he says where treasure, we come back to.

'I hoped you would be able to explain the message in the painting.' said Ben confidently.

Leonides went on to say that the explanation was probably lost somewhere in his family archives. Or maybe that it was the sort of secret that could only be related by word of mouth. The one member of his family who almost certainly knew was George, hence the painting. But the first question to look into was what, if anything, did the treasure consist of? Most of it was likely to be antiquities, looted from churches in the Peleponesse and what we would nowadays call sites of archaeological interest. The problem with antiquities, statues for instance, was their bulk. Transporting them was only part of the problem, hiding them was the really tricky bit. Leonides went on to explain that his instincts ran

contrary to all the historical accounts of the event, which asserted
that the treasure was taken to Thebes, sixty kilometres away, and
buried somewhere there never to be seen again because of the
way the town had been developed. He explained that old Thebes
had been virtually destroyed by massive over-building, making
excavation unthinkable, impossible.

'No, all come back to Parnassos' said Leonides 'good reason
for seeing painting. I think h'e hide statues closer to cave
where h'e kept them. His men haul up big heavy pieces, field-
guns, other things – so statues not a problem.'
No description of what treasure he had, no inventory was ever
found – probably because there wasn't one – but there is no doubt
that he had plenty of stuff.

'Next we look for gold. Gold most interest every one.' said
the sole survivor of Odysseus's line. 'It interest bad men, of
course.'

One of the compelling reasons for listening to the old warrior's
descendent was the way he emphasised almost every word with
wild gesticulations. It was like watching a windmill in a stiff
breeze.

Leonides went on to explain that in the early nineteenth century,
after the Napoleonic wars had been paid for, the English
government in London decided to reduce the interest rate on their
government bonds, leaving the wealthy citizens of that great
financial city looking elsewhere to place their investments.

The answer they arrived at was investments, mostly by way of
bonds, in other foreign governments. Countries like France had
large reparations to pay; so had Austria, Russia and any number of
South American countries, who had been experiencing their own
revolutions. All needed financing. It was an attractive investment

because in effect it was profit with very little risk, for as a general rule countries do not default. Then up pops Greece. This time as well as offering an opportunity for profit, the investment provided an emotional conduit for Hellenism, the democratic ideals of early Greek civilization being widely admired among the educated classes of Europe.

But in London the first loan ran into problems. Looked at objectively, it was a disgraceful exhibition of cupidity and fraud by members of the London Greek Committee as well as the two Greek Deputies in London. The upshot was that the first instalment of this first loan – much reduced by various commissions and pilfering – reached Zante in April 1824 on board an English frigate, the *Florida*. It consisted of £30,000 in gold sovereigns and £10,000 worth of gold double florins from Holland. In the event it got there too late, that is to say it arrived after the death of the famous Commissioner, Lord Byron.

Leonides reminded Ben how much Byron had meant to the Greeks, then and even now come to that. However, because there was no longer a Commissioner in Greece, the question of what to do with the newly arrived gold arose; and the solution, produced like a rabbit out of a hat by the only English banker on the island, one Samuel Barff, was to put the *specie* in his own vault. Typical behaviour for a banker, then as now, thought Leonides, Ben nodding in agreement.

But when news of Byron's death reached London the value of the Greek bonds fell dramatically. The Committee – up to their necks in personal speculation – could not hide the fact that their situation was desperate, and a scandal ensued. Trying to salvage something from the wreck, the Committee sent out two new Commissioners. On their arrival in Zante they discovered that the English banker had by then, and entirely on his own initiative, already forwarded the gold to a representative of the new government, which would have been fine except that the new government didn't exist. It hadn't been formed. But Mr Barff was alleged to have said that "If the money was meant for Greece, to Greece it must go." And it had gone.

The point Leonides wanted to make was that, with all the muddle, the confusion as well as the scandal surrounding the first loan, the existence of the gold had become completely obscured. And with the English banker's eagerness to send the funds to Greece, the actual whereabouts of the gold had become shrouded in mystery. No-one really knew what was going on and it was this obscurity that created an opportunity for one or two of the warlords to step in. It was thought that they did just that.

'Odysseus managed to get his hands on a good part of it.' Leonides paused, unable to disguise his pride at the old devils opportunism. 'He had been fighting for the cause of Greek freedom since 1823, lord of the vast plains he looked out on from his cave, the plains where the Turks and revolutionary Greeks frequently pitched their battles, so why shouldn't he have some of the gold? He felt entitled to it.'

Leonides was now well into his stride. He said it was about then that an Englishman, Edward Trelawny, joined Odysseus in his cave as his sort of Chief of Staff. Trelawny, in fact a Cornishman, had managed to insert himself into the set of English expatriates surrounding Byron and Shelly in Pisa. After Shelly's death, Byron persuaded Trelawny to accompany him on his expedition to Greece. But by the time they got there, Trelawny had grown disenchanted with Byron and his lack of romantic spirit, his seeming reluctance to engage in any kind of adventure. That was when he fell in with Odysseus, and he changed tack, hero-worshipping him instead of Byron. In his eyes, Odysseus was the real thing, a fully blown romantic. He wore outrageous clothes with daggers in his belt, and he had proper moustaches. Trelawny,

99

being one of the world's great fantasisers, found that allegiance to a flamboyant warlord suited him. It enabled him to play the part of corsair, a part he had always fancied. In turn, Odysseus, who had never trusted anyone, came to trust Trelawny, to the extent that he actually married off his very young half-sister, Tersita, to him, and in doing so actually brought him into the Androustes clan.

But problems lay ahead. For another, much larger loan, had arrived and this time it actually reached its intended destination, the newly formed government. And ironically, it was the arrival of the second loan that finally, and fatally, cooked Odysseus's goose. From then on he began to lose influence, and with it power, both having passed – as a result of the bullion's arrival – to the emerging government. So, as was his habit, Odysseus once more decided to switch sides, on this occasion to the Turks. But his luck had run out, and he was murdered.

'Sensing the onset of danger, Odysseus decided to hide his treasure, helped of course by Trelawny. That's how the story of buried treasure started.'

Leonides finished his yarn, looking satisfied but obviously thirsty.

'Ben, remember we go to concert tonight? Well, we must leave or soon be late.'

19.

The programme was unremarkable except for a piece by Berlioz, an extract taken from his Fantastic Symphony featuring an *obligato* for the viola. This was to be played not on the viola but by the orchestra's star cellist, Melina - their only reason for going to the concert. But Melina didn't play. It was her fellow cellist, a young man with the palest of faces, who stepped into her shoes. The small party was deeply disappointed, but changes to a programme do happen at the last minute, and they had no choice but to stay. Their seats were towards the back of the hall, but even at that distance Ben could sense that Melina was pre-occupied. What was troubling her? Why hadn't she played?

Neither Leonides nor Lela were very musical. Leonides, though he could whistle a phrase or two of a well-known tune, couldn't tell a crotchet from a minim. In his experience, music was something you more or less had to put up with, but that didn't stop him tapping his foot to whatever music was on offer, frequently in a quite different time to that of the band or orchestra. On the other side of him, Ben noticed that Lela sat in rapt attention, her eyes never straying from the players in the orchestra.

After the performance they waited for Melina and all four of them went round the corner for a bowl of olives and a glass of wine. Ben and Leonides walked ahead together chatting about Athens, Ben noticing that Lela had fallen into conversation with Melina. The younger woman – as if to emphasise what she was saying – kept turning the palms of her hands upwards in a shrug of despair. At the taverna, Ben seized an early opportunity to ask what was troubling her and she was about to reply when the other two rejoined them. The moment had passed.

Then, out of the blue, Leonides said to Ben that he and Melina should go out for a meal on their own, saying as an excuse that the

101

veterans of the party needed to put their feet up. Turning to Melina Ben saw her lips articulate a clear yes, and half an hour later, they took off in the direction of the *Voudrakis,* a favourite haunt of hers.

oooooo

It wasn't until they had finished their main course that Melina, yielding to an impulse that only those in some sort of distress give in to, leant forward and gripped Ben on his fore-arm. Her lovely eyes, under a brow furrowed with concern, penetrated his calm gaze with disturbing intensity.

'You've spoken to Alex, I know.' she said, 'Now you must hear my story, if for no other reason than there may be a connection between the events of my early youth – at least the man behind them – and what brings you to Athens.'

'Not if it causes you any distress - you know I wouldn't want that.'

'Well, it does a bit,' pausing mid-sentence, her memory of the events clearly still fresh 'but that's beside the point. Although it was a very long time ago, the wound went deep enough never to heal completely - at least so far.'

Neither wanted a dessert, just a coffee and, for the first time in a long while, Ben actually toyed with the idea of a small cigar. It would give him something to do.

'I know Alex told you he is not my father, my real papa that is. He isn't. But I feel for him as though he was. Alex was my saviour, the best father a girl could wish for, loving and endlessly patient. As he will have told you, my father was drowned when I was very young,' she broke off briefly, drawing in a wistful breath, before going on 'and, tragic

102

though that was, it was but the first in a series of misfortunes. My small world, literally, started falling to pieces. Mama was French. For more than six months she kept our little family together, I don't know how, but when you really have to you can find resources hidden somewhere inside yourself. You see, having given her heart to Greece, she decided to stay there and give it a go, never returning to France.

Ben decided against a cigar and opted for a beer. So did Melina.

'For a while' she continued 'Mama managed. But not being Greek and having no family of her own on the island to support her, she was never going to be able to keep going. Island life can be tough on a widow. After a while, another man came into her life, the single most important point in his favour being that he was a local. They didn't marry, their relationship wasn't like that, and all might have turned out well enough, had the man not turned out to be a complete bastard.'

The last word was spoken with startling vehemence. She was forcing herself to dredge up the past, her eyes moist with the unhappiness of long submerged memories. But she wasn't the Melina Ben had first met for nothing. Her response to life was impulsive and total. After a sip or two, she picked up the threads of her story.

' It was a humid, rather dull afternoon in late April. I remember every detail of the day, although I can't have been more than about five at the time. Anyway, I was up on the roof patio above and behind our house. It was a favourite place of mine because you could see the sea - and there I chose to imagine, that with an onshore wind I could catch an echo of my father's voice coming in, returning as it were, with the waves.

Anyway, he suddenly appeared. His name was Zaros

Martanzos by the way. As he approached he began unzipping his flies, fumbling inside his trousers and pulling out his penis. Coming over to where I was sitting he made it obvious by his gestures that he wanted me to do something. I struggled to get away, screaming loudly as I did so and knocking over a table. My mother rushed onto the patio. In her hand she had one of those raffia grocery bags, which must have had something heavy inside. She swung it, hitting him hard in the groin. It was his turn to yell, and he did. We became a very unhappy household, with no way out for anyone. But that wasn't to be the end of it, for out of the blue a month or so later my mother died. Out on the islands in those days there was no doctor, so if you fell really ill, you were very vulnerable. Anyway, at the time no reason was given for her death. It remained a mystery, with the more suspicious islanders pointing a finger at him.'

Apparently that was when Alex stepped in. He scooped Melina up and without wasting a second took her off from the island and away to Athens. There, a friend of his sister, none other than Lela, came to stay with them. It was really she who ensured Melina's salvation.

So that was were Lela fitted in and in an instant it explained the intimacy between them.

'That's why you were able to fall into a deep conversation with Lela on the way from the concert. I saw you, and wondered. Was it about not playing the solo?'

'Partly. I was bringing her up to date with recent events. There were also things she needed to tell me. Ben, the reason I didn't play tonight was that the man I've just told you about, Martanzos, telephoned me in the afternoon. And what really rattled me was that he was enquiring about you; he kept rambling on, in a very unpleasant way. It upset me dreadfully.

By the time he had finished I was a bag of nerves, and in tears. I was in no mood to play.'

Ben had just witnessed the effect his man could have on her. The way he frequently tried to intrude on her life had to stop or one of these days she would sink without trace. Not right now, perhaps, but he needed to find out what this Martanzos fellow had been enquiring about.

'Melina, for someone whose life had been scarred so deeply, you're an incredibly positive person.'

What he was about to add, but thought perhaps he shouldn't, was that Melina had such a natural fondness for getting on with life that she reminded him a bit of Gill.

'I'm looking forward to our expedition, Melina. By the way, Saturday would suit me better; tomorrow afternoon a friend of mine arrives from London. Would it suit you if he came with us? He'll buy his own wine of course. The only drawback is that in a previous life he thinks he was a sailor. Actually, he's a picture restorer. Apart from that he is highly civilised. His name is Cedric Simmonds, but he answers to almost anything.'

'Yes, of course. All the world loves a sailor,' she added provocatively 'me included. He's very welcome.'

20.

'We h'ave ' said Leonides, still struggling with his 'h's,
'visitors for lunch. Bazil Karamanlis, and wife Sue, in Athens
and ask come for lunch. Sue say want to see you not..... me!'

Leonides followed this observation by imitating the whine of a sad
violin. He had come to a halt by the front door shouting the news
backwards towards Ben, who was huddled over a cup coffee.
Ben almost jumped out of his skin. But realising he would have
to leave at the latest by two o'clock to meet Cedric at the airport,
he seemed to have a ready-made line of retreat. Moreover, Bazil
would be there, providing something like a third party insurance.

'Asked Alex join us. He need talk to you and come before the
lunch. H'e say urgent.'

Leonides went on his way out through the front door, leaving Ben
to his coffee. So taken aback by this news, for a split second Ben
even began to wonder whether Leonides might have put some iron
filings in his coffee.

oooooo

Ben's growing sense of unease was the growing number of
phantom-like shadows hovering over the man he knew only as
Martanzos.

An opportunity to learn more about him might come with Alex.
What possible reason did Martanzos have for mentioning Cedric
and him when he was talking to Melina? For heaven's sake, why?
Who could have told him about us? A suspicion was fluttering in
the back of his mind about poor George: could he perhaps have
been the victim – however remotely – of this sinister fellow?

So far he had found being in Greece an invigorating experience, a voyage of re-discovery, mixing in fresh experiences with memories of earlier visits. More recently, though, this old country had started to show him a darker side.

oooooo

Alex showed up by the middle of the morning and suggested that they go for a walk in the nearby park. Setting off in step with each other, their shoulders slightly converging against intrusion from passers by, Alex got to the subject of his concern immediately.

'It's Martanzos' he started 'who is proving unusually stubborn; he seems to be throwing caution to the winds. Whenever, in the past, he has come up on her radar, Melina just lets me know. Because I'm one of the few people who knows nearly the whole truth, quite a lot of detail about his past, when I contact him he readily backs off. That's works and so far that's proved foolproof. I think I frighten him, as I might let the past out of its bag, so to speak.'

As he was speaking he waved his arms up and down excitedly in the manner of his countrymen, though today his arm movements were even more pronounced.

'But...now things are different. The rules have changed.' A puzzled look crossed his face. 'He shows no concern for anything I say and is unwilling to back off. What's up? How has he got wind of you – he mentioned it to me – and he seems very exercised about it.' Alex was clearly troubled by not being able to understand. 'I can't think why. I know he has business interests at Polidoros, a town well beyond the area of Parnassos you're interested in. Yet his problem must be being driven by some connection between you and Parnassos.'

Poor Alex, Ben thought. So often the way – when a formula

always works, and then for some reason it suddenly doesn't, you are stumped. And professors have a horror of being stumped.

'Like an old-fashioned water diviner,' said Alex with mock seriousness 'my piece of willow is twitching. For the time being, my friend, you really must be on your guard. That's as far as I can see, or say. You need to beware, for he is known to be a ruthless man. He may be powerful in that region of the country, but he is not omnipotent. Just keep a good look out.'

Time had slipped by, and they had to turn back. They had to return before the Karamanlis party arrived.

oooooo

'Where you been?' Leonides raised dark eyebrows in their direction. 'Ben, you thirsty?'

'Yes,' said he 'I am. Normally I only get thirsty when I've been talking, but oddly enough this time, I've actually been listening. To the professor, here.'

'I have told Ben of my worries,' said Alex. He and Leonides had obviously talked.
There was a bustle in the hall: first Sue, then Bazil came through and were greeted by Leonides, who introduced them with a general sweep of his arms. Ben noted that Alex was meeting them for the first time.

'Ola!' began Ben warmly, using the wrong language. This was quickly followed by an apology and a timid 'Yassou! That sounds better, Sue?'

'Ben, this is such a pleasant surprise. Very good to see you. You've met Bazili?

108

'Hi!' Tom looked him squarely in the eye 'I don't think we've met, have we? Well not quite.'

'How are you?' the safe reply used by diplomats and politicians when they weren't sure if they had met you before had a more authentic ring to it this time. He seemed really to want to know. 'What do you make of Athens?'

'Look, lets go into lunch....'

Leonides didn't finish. It had been instinct that had told him to keep the party moving.

Leonides led the way out into the courtyard where the sun was guilding the early showing of jasmine in warm gold. He placed Bazil next to himself, Alex the other side, then Ben and Sue facing each other.

'Ben, Leo said you are enjoying Athens, but am I right, you seem preoccupied...' she broke off.

'I suppose I am, just a little. But no more than usual.' His vaguely troubled eyes looked at her agreeing that he might be a bit on edge about something.

'Bazili, I believe you know Zaros Martanzos.' Leonides said enquiringly.

'Yes, I have met him, in Athens I think it was.' Karamanlis remained quite at ease, unperturbed by the out-of-the-blue question from his host. 'Is he a friend of yours?' was his neat response.

Ben was electrified by the short exchange. He had no idea, until Leonides touched on the subject, that Bazili might somehow be involved with Martanzos.

Leonides, catching Ben's eye across the table, mentioned that he'd got a call just before lunch with the news that Cedric's plane had been delayed - arriving that evening at about six-thirty. Bazili, also noticing the time, cut across both of them to say that, as he had a meeting the other side of Athens at three, he would have to get a move on. Thanking Leonides profusely he left the party.

After Bazili had gone Leonides and his guests settled back to nibbling small chunks of what Ben thought must be a sort of feta marinated in a strange variety of wine-red liquor. The conversation rattled away with a noticeably lighter touch until Sue, putting her hand invitingly on Ben's forearm, asked if he would like to see something rather special? Dating from the second century BC it was a tower, she said, waving her arms over her head. 'On its four sides are the oldest recorded depictions of the four wind quadrants - known to Greeks as the άνέμοί.' She felt sure Ben would be interested.

He was, somehow also knowing that it probably wasn't just winds she had in mind. And in less than half an hour Ben and Sue were on their way to where these heavenly air movements had been so keenly observed more than two thousand years earlier. Sue, looking deep into Ben's eyes, said that the old octagonal tower could wait, couldn't it? Her sisters house, where she was staying, was close by the tower and it would be best if they headed straight there.

A maxim of old sailing days - never let a fair wind go to waste - found its way into Ben's brain as they approached the front door. Fumbling for her keys Sue let them in.

'Back in a second' she whispered vanishing along the corridor, and true to her word she glided back into the drawing room a few

110

seconds later, now wearing a loose fitting dressing gown. And not a lot more, realised Ben.

'Follow me *mon brave*' she half whispered, kissing him warmly. Walking on what seemed like cushioned air Ben did as he was bid, turning into what was clearly her bedroom for it was littered with thrown-off clothes. Sue was visibly trembling in anticipation. Barely able to restrain herself, her whole body seemed gripped by an intensity of desire and in little more than a nano-second they were locked in the urgency of an all-consuming embrace. Throwing any thought of decorum to the winds, their appetite knew no bounds until, eventually, they lay back, Sue resting her head on Ben's stomach, her soft hair brushing lightly on his skin. Ben's hands were tracing an arc over the firm shape of Sue's breasts, feeling her nipples harden. Tautening her muscles with renewed need, she slipped her head lower, her mouth ensuring Ben's arousal.

Through a haze of intense pleasure, Ben realised he was actually hearing Sue mumbling something. Yes, she was asking him where they were planning to go when his friend joined him. Ben heard his own disembodied voice replying that they would be going to a village called Tithorea, then up Parnassos to the *Mauve Troupe*. Lying on his back, overwhelmed by the sheer intoxication of pleasure, Ben was enjoying the quaint mixture of liberation and clarity of mind that follows an orgasm. But a mildly anxious thought drifted unbidden across his consciousness *quod omne animal post coitum est triste,* bringing him wide awake in an instant. He knew he must soon be on the road to the airport to pick up Cedric.

On the way there Ben mulled over the conversation at lunch. Leonides's question to Karamanlis about Martanzos had clearly been been prompted by Alex. And what an urbane fellow Sue's husband was – being such a well-trained diplomat it was quite

111

impossible to tell what he was really thinking. Yes, he must be sure to brief Cedric, but he didn't want to frighten him before he had had a chance to find his feet in Greece.

21.

Cedric and Leonides took to each other immediately, which helped make a convivial party that evening, with Cedric telling all sorts of very tall stories about gales in the China seas . Before going to bed they had talked much of the night away.

The morning sky was bright and clear, fine weather heralding the warmer days of spring. Ben thought that such a fine start to the day, like a good breakfast, would make for a day full of promise. It was already full of Cedric, he smiled to himself as they hurried along on the road westwards out of Athens. He had acquired two maps, one of Central Greece, covering the region from Sounion to the Corfu Channel, and the other, a detailed hikers map, of the Parnassos range itself. They shouldn't get lost.

The plan was to meet up with Melina at a place just off the Athens-Corinth road. She had chosen a restaurant overlooking the bay of Salamis, the bay where the Persians and Athenians had fought their celebrated battle two and a half thousand years ago. A curious victory, but an important result, for the legacy of Salamis, as Ben remembered it, was the timeless divide between East and West. Cedric said that one of the problems with naval battles was that all you ever saw was sea, in this case the bay, the straits and an island called Salamis.

Their plan worked smoothly enough and by one o'clock they had found Melina and the three of them had started in on their *kalimares.* It was Cedric's first taste of Greek white wine, and he was heard muttering that ginger ale might improve it. He was obviously quite taken by Melina from the moment they first met. Who wouldn't be, thought Ben. She was wearing a beige cotton smock faced with narrow stripes of dark green silk, the outfit making a striking contrast to her corn coloured hair. Back to her normal self, in love with life, her deep voice booming away, it appeared to Ben that she, in her turn, might just be a little bit taken by Cedric. During the car journey Cedric had come close to exhausting Tom with a detailed account by Themistocles of the winning tactics at Salamis. Tom listened, with only a quarter of an ear, concentrating on the giddy task of driving amid so many furious Athenians. Ben had already briefed Cedric on what he had learnt during his few days in Athens.

Lunch over, and Cedric feeling more charitable towards the white wine of the country, they set off in convoy in the direction of Thebes. Cedric had made a gallant attempt to join Melina in her car, but thanks to Ben's wrecking tactics it came to nothing. About half way there, they turned left off the main road and headed south towards the Gulf of Corinth. This time Cedric succeeded in swapping cars and eagerly climbed in with Melina.

Gently sweeping, brush covered hills rose up on either side of the road, interrupted occasionally by fields of olive trees and a few old oaks. From time to time, small white houses became partly visible, shaded from the afternoon sun by clusters of trees and shrubs. Finally, they rounded a bend in the road and there before them was the Gulf. This last stretch of the Gulf of Corinth is guarded by mountains on the mainland to the north and by mountains to the south on the Peleponesse, until gradually the gulf comes to an end at Corinth itself on the narrow isthmus that connects the Peleponesse to mainland Greece.

The convoy wound its way down and around the last few hairpin bends and there before them was the even brighter blue of the smaller gulf of Alkionides and the inlet behind Cape Lepto that forms the bay and Port of Germenos. Revving high in low gear, they followed Melina up a rough track to the right above the tiny port and in a short while came upon a large but dilapidated house on two floors, fronted by a long veranda. Looked after by an elderly couple from the village, it belonged to the parents of one

114

of Alex's students. They were expected, and here they would be welcome to spend the night amid the decaying splendour of a very old family house.

With a few hours of daylight left, they left their cars in the shade of a porch on one side of the house and went out for an exploratory walk. Melina wanted to show them the remains of a fortress that had stood sentinel on the headland.

Perfectly situated on a bluff overlooking the sea, stands the impressive ruins of the fortress of Aigosthene. Built in the 4th century BC by an ally of Sparta it commands the northern shore of the Gulf. Cedric felt he could almost read the minds of those who had once been billeted there, daily staring out over the gulf in anticipation of danger. What next caught their attention was the sight of a tiny white chapel up on the acropolis, well within the perimeter walls. They walked up to it. On the wall facing them, in Greek lettering, were the words Ayios Yeoryios, or St George. As she opened the old oak door, creaking on its hinges, Melina said that it had been built long ago during the Byzantine era. Inside, the walls were decorated with crumbling frescoes. By the door hung a frayed bell rope running up to an insecure looking bell suspended above the entrance. The bell was suspended from a small arch, with a white stone cross on top of it. If any building had spirit of place, this had to be it.

Along the Gulf of Corinth, beyond the limestone bulk of Parnassos, the sun was sinking in the western sky - in the measured words of Tennyson 'the baths of all the western stars'. A romantic setting, that evening it seemed especially magical to all three of them.

It was now time to return to their ramshackle old house and start thinking about dinner. Melina was showing Cedric one last detail of the Orthodox Church's obsession with icons just inside the tiny porch entrance. Ben had gone ahead on his own, walking along the stone perimeter wall. Coming to a gap in the wall, which long ago might have been an arched entrance to the fortress, he stopped. Immediately outside the line of the wall, the level ground was grassed over and there he saw a circle of stones, flat stones no bigger than the size of a man's hand, which had been set into the grass at regular intervals. To his astonishment, they marked out a Greek letter, the letter that had been haunting him for the last few days. It was the letter **Φ**. About a metre and a half across, you could never miss it.

Awestruck by this ominous reminder of his reason for coming to Greece, he hadn't noticed that Melina and Cedric had come up behind him. Cedric immediately saw what had stopped Ben in his tracks and bent over to take a closer look himself. Melina on the other hand knew exactly what it was. She took Ben by the elbow and following the curve of the letter with a flourish of her hand, she said

'That's the Greek letter, Phi. Put there, I should think, by a member of the *philiki* many years ago. Very few are left now.

'What was it for?' said Ben.

'It probably marked a meeting place, for a local group of the *Philiki Eteria.*'

'And roughly what sort of date would that be?'

'It could be as recently as World War II, when Greece was occupied by the Germans; or it could go all the way back to the eighteenth century. As you can see, it has been damaged over the years….' Her voice had trailed away, lost in her own thoughts.

116

These stones weren't recent, that much he could easily see. Neither did they seem to be nearly two hundred years old, making the second World War the favourite, thought Ben. He would have to goad Melina into telling him more, perhaps over dinner. And although he had spent much of the day with Cedric, he hadn't yet found the right moment to fill him in on all his discoveries, including Melina's background. He must be sure to do that, sooner rather than later the way things seemed to be going.

oooooo

All three were sitting in comfortable wicker chairs on the veranda as dusk fell. Around them the shrubs and trees in the garden began to morph into mysterious shapes distorted by the onset of darkness. A kerosene lamp on an old iron table threw weird shadows onto the little patch of cut grass. Cedric, with a can of beer in front of him, wanted Ben to know with what pleasure he was drinking something that didn't taste of cough medicine.

Ben remembered that Leonides had said that no-one must know about the painting; but did that include Melina? He had said absolutely *no-one*. And since he obviously meant what he said, Ben felt certain he should not involve Melina in any discussion about it, not for the time being. So be it. But they could talk about the *Philiki* with impunity.

The residual warmth from a long day of hot sunshine had all but gone, and the cool of the evening told them it was time to seek a meal in the small port. Melina leading, they found the descent easy, and in no time had settled on the restaurant by the jetty, the Akrotiri. It was too cool to sit outside, so they chose a table inside in the corner. Being on the Gulf, it was principally a fish restaurant and they settled for *bakaliaros*.

Cedric was so smitten with Melina that at first he offered to share

117

a chair with her – which wasn't what he had meant to say at all.
He was speaking with the confusing doggerel that the English
sometimes fall to using when addressing foreigners. Covered
in confusion at the gaffe, he made up for it by saying what a
great day they had had, and what a wonderful welcome he was
having to Greece. Raising his glass to the success of their quest,
he clinked it against Melina's in a gesture of gratitude. They had
moved onto red wine, Cedric muttering that the first bottle had
done little to drown the death rattle.

'Melina,' said Ben 'you seem to know quite a bit about the
philiki?'

'Yes, I suppose I do.'

Momentarily startled, but realising his interest was genuine she
looked for the right words before continuing

'Like all Greek children, we were force fed on the subject
of Greece's Revolution, you know, against the Turks. And
the *philiki* played an important role in the struggle, a key
component to its success. They weren't a bunch of scatty
romantics. You should ask Leo.' She broke off almost in mid
sentence.

'Yes,' said Ben 'what I'm thinking about is the section of
the *Philikoi* that subsequently turned away from the original
brotherhood and its ideals, but using the structure of a secret
society for their own, it is thought criminal ends.'

Once again Melina appeared surprised, almost uncomfortable.
Drawing a deep breath she looked straight at Ben, and continued
in a markedly softer tone of voice

'Remember the story of my childhood, Ben?'

Ben nodded, fearing what might be coming. A wave of sympathy for the oppressed little figure sitting across the table engulfed him; all he wanted to do was wrap her in that missing layer of protective affection she craved for. And, yes, he hated persecuting her with yet more questions – it was too like treading on broken glass.

'Would it surprise you to learn that Martanzos is an active member of the *philiki*? The wrong one, of course…' she felt unable to finish, looking forlorn, so desperate to leave it all behind.

' Anyway, he is. I know very little about this part of his life. As you know from the other evening, from time to time he contacts me, and I have an arrangement with Alex: I let him know immediately, and he takes care of it. It was Alex who warned me many years ago that Martanzos was embroiled in their murky affairs.'

The meal had been just what they needed, and it was time for a breath of fresh air. Walking slowly along the shoreline before the short climb up to the ramshackle mansion, it was evident to Ben that Cedric and Melina might appreciate being left to themselves. So he lengthened his stride imperceptibly, leaving them their own space.

In the morning Melina would be heading back to Athens, at least for a day or two, possibly less, thought Ben with a smile. Meanwhile he and Cedric had plans for their excursion to Mount Parnassos, keen to see the reality of their picture. And Ben, being something of a mountaineer, had an added reason to look forward to being in the mountains again, because up there in the mountains he knew he would feel the solace of home.

He often wondered what it was about mountain ranges, that they so effortlessly lifted one's spirits? Casting your eyes on them you immediately feel restored; your imagination could imitate the eagles, sweeping and gliding through the invisible mountain air. Apart from being remote places where the ancient Greeks tended to keep their Gods, mountains also provided a humbling experience for those who climbed them. Ben was quite sure everyone felt better for being among them, including the restorer. But he wasn't sure, as Cedric appeared to have focussed his mind on other things.

22.

At breakfast, Cedric announced he was beginning to feel quite at home in Greece. He had woken up after dreaming about an earlier life listening to the bouzouki and the yearnings of the great Theodorakis. All very well, he said to Ben and Melina, even if you accepted that music was one of the key discriminators of a civilised society; but it left unanswered the vexed question of what to eat and as importantly what to drink first thing in the morning. He felt in no doubt that breakfast should follow the sensible English tradition of a meal worth getting up for, and that at the very least the coffee should be drinkable and not something you might want to put into the gear-box of a car belonging to someone you would rather wasn't your neighbour.

'What is this absurd *yahout* stuff?' Is it for cleaning windows?'

'Very good for windows, very good for you!' said Melina patiently, rolling her eyes in Ben's direction. 'Where has he been all these years? In a zoo?'

'Not quite house-trained for a zoo,' Ben apologised 'though we've been hoping for some sort of response to a series of high voltage treatments.'

They said their good-byes and Cedric obviously meant it when he said 'soon'. Melina would phone to let them know when she would rejoin them.

oooooo

The road took them westwards through Thebes, a hill-top town that had buried all traces of its ancient and courageous past. Then on past Livadia, a mill town for the region's cotton growing, and a few miles later they caught the first hint that the land further west was rising. Here the road split: to the left towards the Gulf of Corinth and Delphi, to the right towards Tithorea. They took the

121

right fork. Soon they began to see the splendid, growing massif of the Parnassos range itself, in Byron's youthful words 'soaring snow-clad through its native sky, in the wild pomp of mountain majesty.'

At Tithorea Kato, or Lower Tithorea, they stopped for petrol and a cup of coffee in the café adjoining the petrol station. Cedric tried asking for a large cup of regular coffee, not the small traditional Greek coffee that to him was like drinking sieved mud. He ended up with two large cups of Greek mud; serve him right, thought Ben, when in Greece drink as the Greeks do. He gazed admiringly up at the thrilling panorama of the Parnassos range.

Back on the road, and in less than a mile they took a ninety-degree turn to the left to begin the ascent to the old walled village of Tithorea itself. Half way up the narrow winding road they came to a cross-roads. To the left was a steep road leading up to a monastery high up on a plateau to the left of the gorge. They took the right turn and briefly drove down a steep decline to a bridge that crossed the river at the bottom of the gorge. The road then rose steeply, narrowing as it climbed, winding its way through ancient stone ruins at the beginnings of the village.

The square in the middle of the village had an immense old oak tree at its centre, with a diameter of two metres. It was here at the village's only taverna that the local community gathered. After a drink at a table in the shade of the tree, they decided to stretch their legs. From the village the smaller road ran upwards between neat lines of small white painted houses. They walked up, gradually gaining height until they reached a small church. The added height had broadened the view, making an impressive panorama.

Above them loomed the awe-inspiring north face of Mount Parnassos, though at the level of the village the mountain consisted mostly of rocky outcrops interspersed with areas of pasture. Well above the village a spur ran out from the shoulder, creating shelter for a wide stretch of pasture. In front of the small church was an open space enclosed by wrought-iron seats and a wrought-iron fence. Beyond these was an eerie void, for the land gave way to a deep gorge. High sided, with a sheer drop of about two hundred feet, the gorge was a vast swathe cut out of the face of the mountain. Known as the Velitza gorge, it had been hewn out of the mountain by torrents of water and ice over æons of time. Running along the bottom of the gorge was a dried up river bed, in winter a gushing torrent of melted snow and ice, in summer barely a dribble. The remains of an ancient paved way could still be seen at intervals along the river bed, tracing its way from the very old village of Tithorea over Parnassos to Delphi. The local name for the river was *Karakoreme*, or Evil Stream. Ben thought the name suited it.

Then, near the railing, he noticed a statue. It was a bronze, larger than life, of a strong, handsome man in flowing garments, it had been placed with care so that it faced outwards, looking out over the gorge and, beyond it, the plain. On the base of the plinth, in rough-cut letters was ΟΔΣΣΕΥΣ ἈΝΔΡΟΥΤΣΟΣ , which Tom deciphered as Odysseus Androustes. We have arrived, he thought. Cedric joined him, nodding his approval as he too recognised the statue.

'A good looking man' said Cedric ' strangely like Byron, don't you think, Ben?'

Gazing out over the plains he had once ruled as a war-lord, his sightless eyes seemed to echo Ozymandias's embittered gasp of despair on the futility of fallen rulers. Ben was prompted to remember that Odysseus had ended his days, hanging from a tower on the Acropolis in Athens.

123

'Those must have been brutal times.' he said, almost muttering to himself. 'In his own way Odysseus was one of the few real heroes of Greece's struggle for Independence. And, ironically, it may have been our generosity with funds that finally ended his life.

'Well, it's this old gentleman's booty we are after.' Cedric sounded thoughtful. 'It's somewhere up there,' pointing skywards to the blue above them.

'Let's go back to the square and find some accommodation for the next few days.'

Ben led the way back down the narrow road and soon they were at the bar of the taverna. In less than the time it took to order a drink, they had been given the name of a local man who owned an apartment in an old house close to the square. The apartment consisted of a large room with a mezzanine built into the rear wall, which had a bed in it. Off the main room they found another bedroom and bathroom. It would suit them well. Fetching their bags, the rolled up painting and maps, they took up residence immediately. Their first action was to unroll the painting, which confirmed to a degree what they had been looking at earlier. But not exactly, for the viewpoint of their painting had to be much higher up.

The skiing season had been over for nearly three months, and a cursory inspection of the folk in the square revealed that there were probably few to be found in the village who didn't actually live there. Just off the square they found a gem of a restaurant. It was tiny, there was only one man in it and he owned it. There seemed little point in asking for a menu, so they conveyed to him that they would have whatever he gave them. That decision turned out to be a good one, for what they were given was *klephtico* – roast venison with rigani, and many of the other herbs that grow in profusion on the lower slopes of Mount Parnassos.

Tomorrow they would find their way up to the plateau, which ran upwards beneath the escarpment, ending at the top with a meadow. They had already noticed that the north face of Parnassos was dotted with several caves, a few small ones here and there, a square one and one or two quite big ones all of which could be accessed from the meadow. Unlike these, the cave they were looking for would be at least sixty feet from the ground. It had been there for as long as anyone could remember, having been a place of refuge from time immemorial. In the 1820's there had been a small guard-house at ground level, where the first in a linked chain of three iron ladders fastened to the rock wall led up to just below the floor of the cave. The house had disappeared long ago. With these pointers to help identify the cave there should be no difficulty in locating the right one. Ben recalled a passage from the hikers guidebook that the cave 'was a hard hours climb from Tithorea' so they must try to leave early in the morning. Should they take a few slices of dried meat and a bit of bread with them? And wouldn't Cedric be calling for a beer? Of course he would, nodded Ben emphatically. Of course.

Scrambling over a hallowed mountain on a treasure hunt had much to commend it. 'Where ere we tread 'tis haunted holy ground' from Shelly's Hellas had only recently kindled Ben's imagination; to turn these embers into a roaring fire he needed a break-through, he needed a message to leap out from the painting.

oooooo

The sky dawned pale orange with wisps of high cirrus along the western horizon; they would need to keep an eye on the weather. Ben and Cedric, up early, ferreted about for some rations to pack into the rucksacks they had found the previous evening at the only shop in the village.

They left the village on the path that started close to the church, the path dropping down to begin with through a gully onto a well defined track which led upwards across a broad meadow. The passage down the steep gully slightly unnerved Cedric, who wondered whether it had been wise not to bring any brandy, even Greek brandy, in his haversack. Once on the meadow the climb began and soon the ascent required all his concentration.

The gorge scoured its way up the face of the mountain, cutting a deep swathe into the limestone, leaving on either side tall walls of bare, white rock. Perched on a plateau on the far side stood the monastery. With cypress trees standing as sentinels around the cluster of buildings it was a picturesque sight; like many structures placed so high up a hillside, its remoteness gave it a timeless quality.

Above the monastery rose the massive slab of mountain called the Lycoura, or Wolf Mountain. So called not only because of the wolverine shape to its head, but also because in the dawn of time when this part of Greece flooded, the inhabitants fled up the mountain to avoid drowning and were pursued by wailing wolves. Cedric couldn't help wondering why they hadn't built an ark, like that sensible old man, Noah. To the right of their path, the meadow rose gradually, then more steeply as it met a nearly vertical escarpment several hundred feet high. By now there could be no doubt you were on a mountain.

In the distance the imperial summit of Mount Parnassos reached for the sky. Rising well above the shoulders of the mountain, the summit cast a brooding presence on everything below. It was here that the path ran closer to the edge of the gorge, where, looking down, it was still possible to catch a glimpse of the rock strewn bottom a further two hundred feet below. The path, etched into the slope by long usage, was little more than three or four feet wide; its surface appeared to be a mixture of light soil and worn limestone, sometimes resembling the colour and texture of marble.

126

Ben and Cedric made reasonable progress traversing the slope and it wasn't long before the path grew steeper, snaking up the hill between fallen boulders of grey, weathered rock. After one of these twisting climbs, the path again followed the line of the gorge, at times getting uncomfortably close to it. They were now walking through rather thicker green, often thorny vegetation. The pathway was clear, but in places the vegetation was beginning to encroach on it. Brushing aside the thorny branches, Cedric was glad they were wearing long trousers. Then the climb became even steeper and he could hear his heart beating louder and louder, protesting at the exertion.

They had been climbing for more than an hour when the path suddenly opened out onto a lush green meadow, a nearly level piece of land ideal for grazing cattle.

To their left stood a water trough. On their right, in the distance, they could just make out the shape of a small chapel, a white building with a cross on the apex of the roof. Beyond the chapel was a grove of oak trees. They staggered across the meadow towards the shade of the trees, removed their rucksacks and perched on a rock. The climb had been a lot harder than they had expected and as if to prove the point their shirts were drenched with sweat.

ooooooo

Cedric had the dazed look of someone who would rather not have been where he was. His eyes had taken on the imprint of distant terror, exaggerated perhaps by exhaustion.

Ben was searching his mind for some half-remembered lines of Auden. Yes, he had a feeling a cat came into it:

.....for an un-catlike
Creature, who has gone wrong

127

Five minutes on even the nicest mountain
Are awfully long.

Some rough bread, torn from Ben's loaf, and a few meagre slices
of salami provided some much needed nourishment for Cedric, as
did a can of beer. The climb had been more than he had bargained
for. Prancing about, miles above sea-level, was not a pursuit for
sailors, certainly not for him. How were they going to get down?

As compensation for the hardship of the climb, the view from
where they were sitting was breath-taking. Behind them the high,
striated wall of rock rose vertically for hundreds of feet above
the meadow, to an extent enclosing it, affording good protection
from the prevailing wind. Dotted along its face were two or
three small caves, accessible from the level of the meadow. In
front, looking out over the Boeotian plains, the distances became
incomprehensible, stretching away from them for as far as the
eye could see. The gorge meanwhile continued winding its way
upwards from unseen depths below. On the other side, rising
steeply to its summit was the so-called Wolf Mountain. Last of all
they saw, at the high end of the meadow and well above ground
level, a large dark recess. It could only be their goal, the *Mavre
Troupe.*

Ben pulled the rolled up copy of their painting out its tube, which
he had tied to the neck of his rucksack. He unrolled it with great
care, as though it had been a scroll from the Dead Sea. The
landscape was beginning to make sense, even though the artist
could never have been able to paint the landscape from anywhere
near here; the perspective had to start from well out over the
gorge – in a sense the painter would need to have been in a hot
air balloon. What he had succeeded in capturing, with his mind's
eye, was a wide panorama of a large section of the mountain: yet,
somehow, he had managed to focus on the part of it they were
now on. It occurred to them that if they went all the way up the

meadow, then turned to look back down to where they were at the moment, they would get an idea of where the buildings may well have been.

Having had a break with time to recover their strength, they shouldered their rucksacks and began the less arduous walk up the meadow towards the cave. Within thirty minutes they were getting close enough to the foot of the face where, like an eerie, the cave looked out from some sixty feet above them. They were now close enough to see holes drilled into the limestone, which they guessed must have been for ladder fixings. These zigzagged, first right then left, to just below the front of the cave. Here the ladder fastenings stopped at an opening that seemed to go into the cliff itself, perhaps to house an entrance, maybe to a trap door giving access the floor of the cave just above.

After staring up at the cave for a few minutes, Ben and Cedric turned to look back down the plateau in the direction of the chapel and the oaks. It slowly dawned on them that near the tiny church, the rocks were distributed in patterns unlike other parts of the meadow. Ruins perhaps? It was hard to say; they would need to investigate.

While gazing down towards the chapel, they caught sight of a man. Cedric described him as 'rum looking', which he certainly was. Wearing dark clothes, with a small domed hat, possibly woolly, he was lurking behind the small white building in a manner which suggested he wanted to remain out of sight. Not the sort of behaviour they would have expected in this remote spot.

Knowing they would return later to the big cave, they decided to make their way down to investigate the ruins in the area beyond the church, and possibly check up on the man they had spotted. The walk down was – comparatively speaking – a pleasure, like turning your back to the wind. Indeed some aspects of the descent were more like an effortless glide, but these were fleeting moments. Soon they came to the place where they suspected a handful of buildings might once have stood. And it was possible to see, without being too fanciful, that the pattern of the ruins – for that was what they were – did have shapes to them, mostly rectangular and in a more or less linear layout. They could make out three, possibly four of them. And, slightly away from the main cluster, they spotted one more.

Not that they were in any way searching for him, there seemed to be no sign of the man. He had vanished into thin air. But he could wait. The question was how closely did these buildings relate to the painting? Reassuringly enough, the number of buildings turned out to be exactly as those shown in the painting. What about the little white cross?

'Had it been you,' he had turned to Cedric 'having just come down from the giddy heights of that eerie, possibly suffering from vertigo, where would you chose to bury your hoard of treasure?'

'Not just vertigo, Ben, in my state it would be terror. Sailors don't do heights. They function at sea level, where common sense is known to prevail. Did you know that St. Teresa of Avila was the patron saint of common sense? Obviously she wasn't the patron saint of mountaineers. But to answer your question, when you bury treasure you have to follow a golden rule, you must hide it where no-one would expect to look for it.'

'You can't mean the ceiling.' Ben replied, waving an arm across the sky.

'O course not.' said Cedric testily'I mean pretty well the opposite. In a close-knit community like this, made up of shepherds, one or two sheep, some womenfolk and possibly the odd nipper, where would you want to spend the least amount of your time? That is to say, other than for doing what nature intended you to do?'

'You mean what the Victorians called a public necessary house? A communal privy.' Ben was gazing at Cedric in admiration. 'You're a genius. That's a very smart idea.'

'It has to be worth a try. What we should be looking for is a building on its own, a judicious distance from the others…..'

Ben made his way towards the isolated ruin they had spotted earlier. He stopped, eyeing the way the rocks fell, trying to see if he could recreate a shape from the derelict throw of stones. Various patterns took on a life of their own as he studied the possibilities. And just then he noticed the time.

They had better not leave it too long or they would be struggling homewards in the dark. The weather, too, was possibly closing in a bit; clouds, swirling banks of cumulus were beginning to tumble over the shoulder of the mountain from the west. He felt sure Cedric wouldn't enjoy going down the mountain without being able to see where he was putting his big feet. They had to get going soon.

Standing close to where the first stones of what they took to be an outhouse lay, they peered quizzically at the pattern, trying to establish a possible layout. Ben shoved his foot against the longest of the stones. To his surprise, it moved. And there, only partly visible, lay the remains of what looked like a very small leather bag with a leather drawstring. He bent to pick it up, but as he did so it seemed as if it might disintegrate. He paused, wondering what to do. The temptation overcame him and he carefully picked up the decaying leather pieces, and held them up for Cedric to inspect.

'An old purse, I should say,' adding 'for keeping coins in.'

Instinctively both of them dropped to their knees to take a closer look. Tom reached for a twig and began, gingerly at first, to scrape around the imprint of the stone. He drew the twig backwards and forwards across the damp earth, but to no avail. Then, a second or so later, there was a small but firm obstruction to the twig's movement. He put his hand on the spot and rummaged around with his fingers in the soil, stopping abruptly on feeling something hard. He pulled his hand away slowly, and there nestling between his forefinger and thumb was a small coin. He rubbed it, then poured water over it from his plastic bottle to get the worst of the soil off. Finally, he wiped it clean with his handkerchief.

The coin was English. George IV's easily recognisable head, crowned with a laurel wreath, suggested a date around the 1820's. Turning it over he saw a relief depicting St George mounted on a horse, sword in hand, lunging at a dragon. It had to be a sovereign. A look of astonished delight came over Ben's face.

'My dear Cedric, take a peep at this little beauty – Are any more?' He was ecstatic. 'I do hope so.'

'Only one way to find out' said Cedric, already on his knees, running his fingers through the damp soil, just like Ben had only seconds earlier.

Seconds later, and exactly like Ben, he stopped abruptly; then, slowly, he continued exploring with his fingers until there, cradled in his palm, were two coins. After brushing the same area of soil backwards and forwards for a few more minutes Ben found one more. That was it. Both were elated at their good fortune. Cedric extended his hand, offering the two gold pieces to Ben.

'No,' said Ben 'they're yours, finders....'

Replacing the long stone, they gathered up their rucksacks and prepared for the return journey. They needed to get going. Ben led the way down towards the lower end of the meadow, and in little more than twenty minutes they were entering the patch of scrub and trees close to the edge of the gorge. Here the path narrowed, the scrub having grown over part of it, and once again they were grateful for the protection of long trousers.

It happened quickly. Ben, in front, was walking at a reasonable pace. He could hear Cedric behind him, from time to time cursing at the thicket when it brushed his arms or legs. Suddenly, there was a whoosh from behind and in a dark flurry of movement something shot out from behind a shrub and crashed into what must have been Cedric, who let out a muffled cry. Ben turned to find an empty space. No Cedric.

He scanned the nearest scrub, spotting a gap in the foliage with bits of broken twigs on the ground. He also took in, instantly, that the distance between the path and the edge of the ravine had closed to no more than about three metres. Christ! He couldn't have! Ben's mind was whirring, his brain accelerating with alarm. Getting a grip on himself, with the alert coolness of a proper mountaineer he moved deftly towards the edge of the gorge. It fell away vertically for at least two hundred feet. He was looking down into a deadly void.

Stepping back from the chasm, Ben edged slowly backwards to scan the short, scuffed track towards the edge, when, to the right he noticed the body of a man, his head turned away. He was a foot or so lower on a narrow shelf at the very edge of the ravine, holding on by an arm through the root of an old tree. It was unmistakably Cedric. Thank God! Ben muttered incoherently.

'Cedric, are you all right?' unintentionally the question was half whispered, his throat dry with shock.

133

'No I'm not.' he replied, pointing towards the awesome drop with his free hand.

'Don't move, Cedric. Not an inch.'

The situation was perilous. Ben, having instantly grasped the true nature of their predicament, knew exactly what he had to do. He began rummaging around inside his rucksack for something he knew was there. Without taking his eyes off Cedric for a second he soon found a short length of climbing rope. White, with red stripes running through the lay, it was soft, and exceptionally strong. Leaning over cautiously, he handed Cedric the rope's end.

'Take this. Whatever you do, don't let go of that root; keep one arm through it and pass the rope half way round your body, then swap your arms over and pull the rest of the rope through until it has gone completely round you.'

Ben watched Cedric following his instructions to the letter. The rope was now all the way round Cedric's body. But it needed to be tied.

'Before you tell me, Ben, I'll tie a bowline on the bight of the rope. The sort of knot we shell-backs do in the dark with our eyes shut.'

Cedric was recovering, however slowly. His old self was still there, alive, and with luck still kicking. Kicking enough, for Ben thought he had heard Cedric say that his timbers had been shivered. Slowly Cedric passed the rope over itself and back up again forming the start of a bowline. He did it perfectly, able to use both hands, but keeping one of his arms threaded through the root of the tree. Meanwhile, Ben had retreated to the upper part of the bank and had passed the other end of the rope round the neck of a rock in order to be able to jam it. Pulling the rope taught, he explained that he would keep it taught until he was on dry land, so to speak. Ben then called to Cedric telling him to start crawling towards him. After an uncannily quiet interval, Cedric gradually appeared, on all fours. He looked shattered.

'Ben,' he croaked. He had to pause, taking a deep breath, before continuing 'A man – very likely the man we saw earlier by the church – jumped out of the bushes and ran at me, pushing me towards the ravine. We tumbled down here and I just managed to grab hold of the root. Thank God. He must be a complete goneburger.'

'For sure.' said Ben. 'That would be a hell of a fall, and onto rocks. Whatever did he think he was doing? He can only have been trying to kill you.'

'I didn't get a look at him – not sure I would want to! But see, I've got his hat.' He stretched out his arm and there in his hand was a dark blue woolly hat.

Sitting on the rocks by the side of the path, it was a good twenty minutes before Cedric had recovered enough to contemplate continuing the descent, and it was not until he was properly on his feet again that they cautiously resumed their journey. Few words were spoken, and then only to confirm slight alterations in direction. Eventually, when they had reached the square, Cedric collapsed at the nearest table, imploring Ben to bring him a horse's neck.

"Brandy and ginger ale, for the love of God! Soda if there's no ginger.'

23.

In the event it was soda. After Cedric's second glass they returned
to their digs and as the shaken mountaineer wallowed in a hot
bath he kept on hoping that the brandy might soothe his nerves
a little. An hour later he was on the phone to Melina, giving
her a misleadingly edited version of the afternoon's events, but
leaving his account with a well judged frisson of danger in it to
elicit her concern. Telling Cedric that she would be in Tithorea by
lunchtime the following day, she implored him to take more care.
Charmed by the warmth of her concern, Cedric made no attempt
to conceal his enthusiasm for seeing her again. He would be in the
square, waiting.

' The question is, should we let Leonides know what's been
going on?' said Ben, already knowing the answer. 'In case we
need help reporting what has already happened, in case we run
into more trouble, I think there can only be one answer: we
must contact him.'

'I'm not so sure.' Cedric spoke slowly, choosing his words
carefully. 'Melina will be with us tomorrow. Her intuitive
response to these events could be all we need; she'll know
how to go about informing the police without involving us in
days of red tape. Wouldn't it be better to wait and see what she
has to say?' He sounded confident, sure he was right. 'Slightly
changing the subject Ben, I have been wondering how on
earth anyone could know we would be *in situ* yesterday; how
could they know we were in Greece, let alone up a mountain?
Telepathy perhaps?'

Someone obviously did know. Ben had been thinking along
similar lines, turning over in his mind some of the details of the
episode, each leading back to the same question. How could *they*
have known? The only people in Athens who knew they were in

Greece were Leonides, Alex, Melina and the girls at the School. Of course there was also Lela – wasn't she privy to everything going on? It certainly looked as though there had been a leak.

Ben stopped dead in his tracks. He was hearing an echo of Sue's voice, questioning him about where they were going. My God, was that it? Could he have been that stupid? It had suddenly become all too horribly clear to him- it was Sue who had asked him, wasn't it? She knew. At the same time he also saw that from Cedric's point of view, keeping Melina out of the loop was no longer an option. No, of course it wasn't, even Ben could see that.

'Cedric, as far as I can see the only people who know we are here – in Greece, as well as on Parnassos – are Leonides, Alex, Melina, Lela and the girls at the British School. And Sue and her husband Bazili. No-one else, is there?'

'Not that I can think of.' Cedric couldn't think of anyone.

Ben was remembering Sue Karamanlis. What a complete idiot he had been; it might have proved a total disaster. What was her husband, Bazil, up to? How was he implicated?

He would also like to know, but didn't dare ask, whether Cedric would ever want to climb up Parnassos again. For the time being, he thought it best to duck the question. He only knew that this evening they must have a meal fit for an intrepid climber.

He reached into his pocket and pulled out the coin that had been nestling there. In the palm of his hand it was small, but because it must be pure gold it had to be worth at least its own weight in that valuable mineral, and old sovereigns were also collectors' items, so it was probably worth very much more. Would they find others? And anyway, what sort of size was an old gun-powder tin? Full of sovereigns, even if it only measured two feet or so by a foot, it would be worth a fortune.

Parnassos! Ever since his school days the name had conjured up a remote land of myths and music; Apollo, with the nine daughters of Zeus singing about the origins of the world and the glorious deeds of past heroes. For Ben, mountains had an almost spiritual quality, they were the last uninhabited wildernesses beyond the reach of civilization. Four lines from Flecker summed up their remoteness:

'Beyond that last blue mountain barred with snow…
White on a throne or guarded in a cave
There lives a prophet who can understand
Why men were born…'

Once the centre of the known world, Parnassos was associated with all the more charming aspects of myth. High on its slopes it was thought one could still catch 'fragments of far off melodies', hummed no doubt to a golden lyre. True, the cave that interested them was on the wrong, the north face of the mountain. On the far side, on a narrow plateau, nestled Delphi, whence the whole world had once beaten a path to consult the Oracle. And above Delphi lurked another cave, famous in antiquity for being home to the Muses, the arts of poetry, music and learning. Ben could only remember one of the nine, Terpsichore, the muse of choral song - because of his love of singing and because the word featured in the motto of his college choir.

Of course their reason for being on the mountain had nothing to do with any of that. It was plain and simple curiosity, but nonetheless a force to be reckoned with. He had been hooked by the mystery of the painting the minute he had seen it, and he hoped it wouldn't be long now before Leonides revealed the full meaning of its last mystery, the small white cross.

138

However, a more disturbing fact had to be taken into account, and it was one Ben had chosen not to pass on to Cedric. He had learnt that the man called Martanzos, knowing they were in Greece, appeared to be neurotic about their intention to climb Parnassos. Had the close shave near the Velitza Gorge been his response? To Ben the answer had to be yes. But he still needed to establish why there was a link between this man's neurosis and their curiosity about Mount Parnassos.

24.

An hour after sunrise the sky over the mountain was clear with just a hint of pink. Another spectacular day was in prospect and Ben had already been for a short run.

He had met nobody, perhaps not surprisingly as his run had taken him up the slopes immediately above the village where the land was relatively level. But on the way back he had noticed a man sitting on a low wall above the road, which led upwards beyond the last few houses of the village. Studying some sort of leaflet, he could well have been in need of knowing how to set the alarm on a new watch. To Ben there was a simpler explanation: he thought they would have been told to keep an eye on the two Englishmen, the ones who had been showing an inexplicable interest in the mountain. It was possible, of course, that he had been told to expect only one Englishman.

Cedric awoke to the aroma of Ben's brew of coffee wafting across his pillow. He shambled over to the sofa announcing that if they had any doubt about their best course of action, the classic way of resolving the dilemma would be to consult the oracle at Delphi, just over there. He waived a languid arm in the direction of the coffee, hoping that Ben would understand his need for a cup.

'Here, help yourself to milk.'

Drawing the line at waiting on Cedric – breakfast in bed would be next – Ben pointed to both the coffee and the milk.

'What time did Melina say she was coming?' he asked, as Cedric poured himself a cup. Reluctantly, Ben noticed.

Ben guessed it would be better if he were absent during their reunion. He already had half an idea of what he might get up to for the couple of hours that lunch might take them, an idea based on heading west.

'She said she would arrive just before lunch, about one o'clock I think. I said we would meet in the square.'

'Perfect. What I suggest is that after we've had some breakfast we go down to Kato Tithorea to look for a shovel. We may also need a picnic bag, or better still a cool bag, for refreshments. It shouldn't take long'

'Good thinking. The cool bag.' said Cedric, cheering up. Cedric was beginning to look forward to the prospect of a glass of something cool, on a handy rock near the remains of their recently discovered village. A beer might answer, but the trouble with beer – he had experienced this too often – was that it was a drink you really only enjoyed in anticipation. When you actually drank the stuff, it tasted well rather disappointingly of beer.

Then, inevitably, he began to recall the frightening episode by the gorge and, uninvited, a reluctance to climb Parnassos again insinuated itself into his consciousness

'I think we should keep any idea of making a plan on hold until we see what Melina has to say, don't you?' he said, looking meaningfully at Ben.

'Fine by me, Cedric.' Half expecting this Ben continued 'Anyway, I don't think we ought to go near the *Mavre Troupe* today' choosing not to use the word gorge, ' we wouldn't have enough time. Unless, of course, I went on my own to take a look while you are meeting Melina.'

'I wouldn't dream of letting you do that,' Cedric was emphatic 'anything could happen up there, and I would be left picking up the bits. Of you!' He broke off, wincing imperceptibly. 'Let's try for a spot of breakfast in the square.'

They strode purposefully towards the taverna, grabbing a couple of chairs in the area under the massive branches. A waiter came out to take their order. In a less obvious a manner, so did another man, choosing a table away from the taverna's door. Within earshot, he sat down with his cup of coffee. No chances, it seemed, were being taking.

oooooo

Ever since he had first opened his eyes that morning, and later while waiting for the kettle to boil, a nagging question prompted by yesterday afternoon's near catastrophe had been getting at Ben. If someone didn't want them on Parnassos, surely all they had to do was to come right out and say so. Given a *good* reason, he thought, we could easily take the next plane home and be done with climbing.

But was it that simple? For the 'someone' who was neurotic about them being on Parnassos was Martanzos. Ben needed to know why this seedy little beggar was so exercised about them hunting for an old warlord's treasure, a few sovereigns for heaven's sake wasn't going to break anyone's bank. And the closer he got to understanding what was going on, a further question popped up. What possible reason could he have for wanting to get rid of them? Try as he might, the sequence of those simple words *get rid of* haunted his train of thought. Being Ben, of course, he needed an answer. His streak of curiosity, now on full alert, had never been more acute. He had to find out, he needed to know what was unhinging Martanzos. That meant he would have to go exploring.

Meanwhile, he and Cedric made the best they could of the ramshackle meal that the taverna tried to pass off as breakfast. And, yes, according to Ben's companion, there was still a problem with the coffee.

25.

There simply wasn't time to go to Kato Tithorea, not for both of them.

'You stay here Cedric, and I'll trundle on down even if it means missing lunch.'

Ben knew he would be better off doing what he had in mind to do on his own; in fact much better off, as Cedric tended to break things, fall over and generally be a bit obvious.

'Fine by me.' intoned Cedric, obviously thinking about something else.

This plan struck Cedric as perfect from all points of his compass. It wouldn't be long before Melina would turn up and he was happy just looking forward to that. And much better with just the two of them. He was surprised by how much he had missed her, and that only after a couple of days. On the other hand he was sure he wouldn't miss Ben.

oooooo

Ben went in search of their hire car and the first thing he did was to reach for the map. Where the hell was this place Polidhrosos? Ah, there it was, about thirty kilometres along a mostly straight road, which ran along the plain between the two ranges of mountains. Driving gently down the hill out of the village in no time he had joined the main road and was making good progress westwards to Amfiklia, where the road kinked sharply to the left before reaching his destination. On either side were scruffy cotton fields where the harvest had long since been reaped, and by the side the road he noticed several wisps of raw cotton stranded in the crumbling wire fence, strands which struck him ominously as an epitome of Melinas's life, wisps too often snagged by the recurrence of tragedy.

Entering Polidhrosos, he soon saw what he was looking for, a petrol station with a sizeable forecourt. Not that he needed fuel, he only wanted to find out where Martanzos lived and he was pretty sure everyone around here must have heard of him.

Pulling in to the garage, he bought half a tank of petrol and went in to pay. Ben was well prepared with his questions, having consulted a pocket-sized dictionary. Pronouncing the actual words proved more of a challenge.

'Καλημέρα!' he said, pausing for effect, if not hoping for applause. 'Νού ονίτι Μαρτανζοσ?'

In asking for the whereabouts of Martanzos's house Ben had shot his bolt. He had given his all, used all his vocabulary in one go. All he could hope for now was a sudden smile of comprehension followed by a few kind words of direction, preferably spoken slowly. But the woman behind the till looked as though someone from the loony bin had entered her shop.

'Τι?' she said.

'Afternoon!' said Ben in the coolest English of the Overseas Service of the BBC
'Martansos house. Where?' This last word demanded an answer. He very much hoped so.

'H'e no leeve here – Ana Polidhroso.' she said, as she did so mercifully pointing up the road. 'Duo kilo' holding up two fingers in case her *duo* had passed him by.

A man came out of the workshop adjoining the forecourt, wiping his hands on his overalls. His wife spoke rapidly to him and pointed to Ben.

'Englees?' Ben nodded. 'Martanzos live *δυο* kilo, big church right side, then climb, soon left big gates. White.'

He didn't look at all pleased to have heard the name Martanzos; it had been the mention of his name that had brought him out to see who was enquiring about Martanzos. With another rub of his hands, this time with a cloth, the man turned his magnificent moustaches away and slouched back to the workshop. Ben had what he wanted, directions to Martanzos's house. Feeling not a little chuffed with his linguistic skills, he thanked the kind woman in the shop and made his way back to his car and onto the road.

He had been told to go straight on through the centre of the town with its twisting and turning narrow streets. In a minute or two he had driven passed most of the buildings, and the town began to thin out. Soon, the town was behind him, and there to the right was a biggish church. Then, and very quickly, he spotted two imposing white gates on the left, with a drive curling up the hill. The gates were firmly closed. They had a forbidding, intimidating appearance. So that's where he lived.

He drove on slowly, seeking a place to stop as soon as possible. On the left, he found a small lay-by. Ben pulled in. He didn't really have a well thought out plan, just to hop over the fence and walk up the drive. Remembering the closed gates and the high fencing on either side of them, he chose instead to climb the hill above the lay-by. It proved a good choice. The climb though steep, and through very dense scrub, began to level off after a while, giving way to grass. He knew well how to scramble through scrub, thanks to many forays into the huge Chaguanas reserve in Trinidad, for as boys they frequently ran wild in that immense jungle. He recalled the sudden fright of putting up a red ibis where the scrub gave way to glistening mangrove.

145

Climbing up, and a bit further to his left, he caught a glimpse of a substantial building. He guessed he must be seeing the structure from the side, which meant he would have to traverse further up to the left. As he got higher he began to see the building again, a large house for that was what it was, but now he was seeing it from closer and looking towards the front. The hill had been excavated in the shape of a giant crescent, cut back from the slope to create a vast swathe of level ground. At its centre was a large, neo-classical house on two floors. Four Doric columns supported an imposing central pediment and wings ran out on either side. The house was a statement about its owner – or the owner's wealth – the overall effect verging on ponderous.

Ben couldn't stand there taking it all in without running the risk of being seen, so he moved quickly over to his right. Approaching the house, he spotted a large sash window on the ground floor. It was shut tight. Working his way closer to it, he could see that there was no-one in the room.

With extreme care, he peered through the window. It was some sort of office, with a large desk and book-shelves running along the inner wall. Standing proud in the middle of the room he spotted a large map of what was obviously a mountain. It could have been an enlarged photograph. It was on an easel, flanked by two others. The shape seemed oddly familiar. Curious, he thought as he stared at it, until it gradually dawned on him that what he was looking was the mountain shoulder immediately above Tithorea, where only yesterday they had been climbing. His first blink of recognition turned on seeing the great black hole near the top. That ominous, but unmistakably cavity was clearly the *Mave Troupe*.

Just then, the quality of the light in the room changed, for the door had opened and three men were entering. The first, dressed in black with a white shirt, stopped near the door holding it by the handle. Ben took him to be a member of the staff, perhaps a butler. Close behind were two other men. The first, he guessed, had to be Martanzos. Although he had never set eyes on him before, he was sure it was him. But the other man, Ben could barely believe his eyes: the taller of the two men was none other than Karamanlis. Talking first to each other and then to the butler, the latter nodded and left the room, closing the door behind him.

The crunch of a foot on gravel over his left shoulder alerted Ben to the peril of his position and, quick as a rabbit, he stepped sideways behind a heavy shrub. Not far from where he was hiding, a man walked past on his way to a parked car. He waited until the car drove off before creeping back to the window. Both men had gone over to the easel and the shorter man was pointing at areas on the map. What a crude looking individual, he thought. The door opened again and the butler seemed to be announcing lunch, for all three left in quick succession. Ben was keen to get inside and see what he could learn from the photograph and other papers. But because it would mean breaking in – literally smashing the window – he thought better of it. Taking his chance to get away he ran across the grass to the start of the scrub. Making his way down the slope he hardly put a foot wrong, arriving slightly out of breath just above the lay-by. There, where he had parked it, was his car. To his sudden alarm, though, he noticed that another car had drawn up behind his and its driver was now standing, leaning over his car trying to get a better look at something inside it. Wearing a kind of working uniform – loose fitting fatigues – Ben thought he might be an off-duty patrol officer, a policeman. So, thinking quickly, he unzipped his flies and started to have a pee - in a very blatant manner and, shouting towards the man, he made it clear that he wouldn't be long. The policemen, apparently satisfied, walked back to his car and drove off.

Back in his own vehicle, Ben breathed a sigh of relief, for the first time realizingthat he must have been a complete nutter to have gone anywhere near Martanzos's house. But he was also exhilarated by what he had discovered. Karamanlis had been lying to Leonides at their lunch: he hadn't met him only once in Athens, he was up to his neck in something directly connected with Martanzos, and his business must in some way relate to the part of Parnassos featured in George's picture. And Ben now knew for sure how their whereabouts was being transmitted to Martanzos. He needed to contact Leonides urgently.

26.

Leonides told Ben that he had made exciting progress in deciphering the picture. But before Ben could ask with what result, an urgent question crackled down the telephone line.

'What have you been doing?' Leonides's voice though gruff, didn't lack warmth.

'We've been going up in the world,' said Ben 'we've been climbing Parnassos. We found the *Mauvre Troupe* and looked round the ruins of the village below it.

'Interesting,' said Ben's former host 'did you say you met someone?'

Certain that he hadn't mentioned anything about meeting anyone, Ben was taken aback. He managed to say

'Yes, we did bump into someone. To begin with he showed a keen interest in our activities, but in the end the poor fellow completely disappeared, nearly taking Cedric with him by the way. How did you know?'

The line went very quiet at his end, almost as if the connection had been lost. After a second, Leonides's throaty voice replied simply that he had heard about it. He went on to tell Ben that he would be joining them first thing in the morning, leaving Athens very early. He hoped to be with them for breakfast at about nine o'clock. They had to be careful, he insisted, from now on very careful.

'Don't do climbing, not more climbing.' He really meant what he said.

'OK. See you tomorrow, early.' he said.

oooooo

Crossing over to the taverna, there, at a discreet table under the umbrella of the oak, he found Cedric and Melina. Unless he was very much mistaken, they looked less than totally pleased with life.

'Hullo you both.' said Ben. He gestured towards Melina with open arms and gave her a welcoming hug.

'Yassou!' the voice from her unfathomable depth boomed 'what have you been doing to Cedric? Didn't I ask you to take care of him?'

'Yes! I did try to look after him.' Ben smiled, 'But he's not an easy person to supervise. He's an energetic child, liable to get lost when out for a walk.'

'Utter nonsense, Ben.' Cedric broke in 'Did you have a successful shopping expedition?'

' Yes, all sorted.'

He had acquired a spade in Amfiklia, having stopped there for a coffee on the return leg of his journey. And a cool bag. When should he tell them about his discoveries?

'By the way, news from Leonides: he'll be with us at breakfast tomorrow.'

By then Ben had taken the remaining chair and, as the waiter approached their table, he glanced round to see what they had been eating and drinking. Their reunion had clearly been

150

celebrated with quite a long lunch. Quite right too, he thought. But despite both of them nattering away, he still felt sure something must be wrong. He plunged straight in.

'What's up?' coming straight to the point, he looked quizzically at Melina with arched eyebrows.

'You tell him, Cedric.' she replied.

'Well.' Cedric started, but stopped dead in his tracts. A man was approaching their table.

In any other place, or in other circumstances, that might not have been remarkable; but Cedric seemed to know exactly who he was, which was certainly unexpected. The man came to a stop, just short of their table, and indicated by a sort of sideways movement of his head that he wanted Melina to join him. Touching Cedric lightly on his shoulder as she rose to her feet, she went over to the man, her head swinging round towards Cedric as if to say 'I told you so.'

The man spoke rapidly, looking at his watch, indicating that a time was being set. He then took his leave, and walked towards his car parked on the far side of the low railing. A minute later he was lost from view as the car headed down between the houses..

Ben was amazed, awaiting an explanation.

'It's alright,' said Melina 'he wants me to see someone at five o'clock this evening. It won't take long.'

'Ben, I was about to tell you Melina's news – the man who has just spoken to her is a part of the deal. Why don't we all have a glass of something?'

Cedric might have been playing for time, or it might simply have been the delayed reaction of a thirsty man. Either way they ordered a beer.

'The problem' continued Cedric 'appears to be a fellow called Martanzos – Melina knew him as a child. I think you know the story.'

'Yes, I do. Very disturbing.'

He waited for Cedric to take a good swig of beer. But it was Melina who took up the running.

'I'm not sure why this has started up all over again, except that it coincided with your arrival in Athens. Normally, I just contact Alex.'

She looked miserable, her past biting her ankle yet again.

'This time it didn't work. And it seems that it wasn't because you had come to Athens, but more your interest in Parnassos that's the cause of the problem. Some long forgotten turmoil in his deranged mind has been stirred up.'

Melina was painfully distraught. She couldn't understand how an episode from a much earlier part of her life could have resurfaced. Cedric shared her concern, and it was touching to see how very much he cared.

'So the person who was here a few minutes ago, came to tell you to be somewhere this evening?' Ben could see where things were heading.

'Yes. I have a date to see Martanzos at five o'clock, somewhere not far from a town near here called Polidhrosos. It shouldn't take long.'

Yes, Ben thought, no more than forty minutes. An idea was taking shape as his mind whirred round.

'I see,' said Ben 'not that far. Cedric could take you in our car if you like.'

'That would be nice,' Melina eyes half closed 'but a car is coming for me. It's not an easy place to find so it's better to have a driver who knows the way.'

Ben nodded. Instinctively he knew that it would be better if Melina should not go on her own to see Martanzos; staring directly at Cedric, desperate to communicate with him, he got no response at all except for a vacaqnt grin on the face of his friend.

Cedric was otherwise occupied. Melina! How can an echo from the past ricochet down the years, tap you on the shoulder and say – hey you! There was no such thing as completely escaping from your past, everyone knows that. He also knew that one of the wonders of the brain was its facility for storing chilling detail. But it didn't always have to be like that, did it? Couldn't he help her start a new life?

He noticed Ben was looking at him rather peculiarly, seeming to need a question answered that he was pretty sure hadn't yet been asked. He also noticed that Ben was in the process of paying, not just for their recent drink, but for their whole lunch. Brilliant! What he fancied more than anything else in the whole world was a short walk with Melina, somewhere among the spring flowers on the meadow above the village.

'Excuse me for a minute, will you?'

It was Ben. Having pushed back his chair, he stood facing them.

'I saw in the shop window down there,' he said pointing towards the corner of the square 'a guide book I would very much wanted to buy. See you later!'

Without waiting for a reply, he turned on his heal and began to wander in the direction of the two or three village shops on the street running down from the square.

oooooo

Ben hadn't made up his excuse: the shop did have a guide, and it had caught his eye on the way to the taverna. The book wasn't for skiers or ramblers, it had a history of the region and notes on its rather sparse economy. Stuffing it in his pocket he continued on his diversionary walk, planning to be back, near the square about half-an-hour before Melina's car came for her.

There was something he couldn't figure out: Zaros Martanzos, possibly thought to have been implicated in the death of her mother – he had no idea if that was true – had summoned her to his house and she had agreed to go? What sort of a hold could he possibly have? She was a brave girl, Melina, and capable. But why should she go?

His idea was to follow her in their car, not closely of course as he didn't need to be shown the way. Cedric had to ask Melina to make sure that the window of his office was open.

Shortly he must be back near the square. He remembered their car was parked on the square itself, actually on the starting grid, so to speak. He wondered if Cedric had ever driven a car; it would be useful if he had, but somehow he doubted it. Not the type.

First he must look up Polidhrosos in his guide. From the index he turned to the page and saw that Polidhrosos was a mining town with very little to say for itself. Much of it had been built since the 1960's when mining for bauxite had properly got going. 'Are you copper-bottoming him, my man? No, I'm aluminiuming him, mum.' The tongue twister wriggled its way into his busy thoughts - an irritating twister, at that.

oooooo

As he was approaching the square he spotted the figure of Cedric, walking in his direction. The picture restorer moved with a lope, his leg movements more those of someone gliding downhill.

'What ho!' he said, sounding crestfallen.

'Melina's gone? Don't tell me she ….'

'Yes, not five minutes ago, in a blue Mercedes.'

'Come on' said Ben ' We have a choice to make.'

They slid into the car, Cedric bemused and protesting, Ben trying to calm him down.
'The point is we can follow Melina – I think I told you I've been there before – and when we are there we can, if they have left the window open, listen to what they say. Did you ask her?'

In fact, Ben was being uncharacteristically reticent. Ideally, he would have liked a further snoop on Martanzos to find out what was really troubling him. The trouble was Ben just didn't relish doing anything like that with Cedric, he simply wasn't cut out for that sort of thing.

'Personally, I don't see any point in doing that, because even if they have left the window open and we can hear them talking, neither of us understands a single word of Greek; and

155

besides, Melina can tell us all about it later. We don't need to run the risk of being caught eavesdropping – you can be sure it wouldn't do her much good if we were caught in the act. So, I think it's a bit of a no-brainer.'

The other option, Ben explained, was to go only as far as Polidhoros, to the garage he had called in on earlier. They could talk to the mechanic, for Ben was remembering how unhappy he had been at the mention of the name Martanzos. He guessed there was more to learn from the man with the fancy moustaches.

'Shall we give that a whirl? If nothing else you will see a the countryside.'

oooooo

They sped along the big main road, past features that Ben was by now familiar with and after a while came to the small town of Polidhoros. There on the right was the filling station with the open doors of the garage behind it. They pulled in. To his relief Ben saw the mechanic coming out and walking straight towards them. Slightly menacingly, he bent down and spoke to Ben through the car window.

'Want now, you want?'

Looking him straight in the eye, with no trace of fear, Ben said

'You no like Martanzos? I see you no like him.' Then, looking pointedly at the mechanic he said simply 'I no like him.'

'Man no-good' he spoke bitterly, through clenched teeth with his moustachios quivering with tightened anger. 'No like, no-good man.'

'We no like Martanzos.' said Ben, including Cedric with a

156

sweep of his arm 'Your name?' he enquired.

'Dimos Drakos,' followed in Greek by a wondrously emphatic 'Σουλίωτξ.' For that brief moment many past generations of Souliotes stood shoulder to shoulder behind this man's proud statement of his identity.

Ben proposed by a gesture of his hand that they walk over to the bar and have a coffee or a beer. Dimos accepted. He was a lean fellow, with strong arms hanging down from rolled up sleeves. His frame was spare and he walked as if, by habit or tradition, he might have been carrying a weapon of some sort.

On the way over to the bar Cedric told Ben that as far as he knew the Suliotes were a tribe from near or in Albania who were renowned for their fighting spirit: the Suliotes had joined the Greeks in their hatred of the Turks some staying and becoming absorbed into parts of Greece after the War of Independence. Spirited fighters, they had defeated much larger Turkish armies sent to subdue them.

Having sat down, the waiter nervously took their order, scurrying away to get it. Ben offered the Suliote his hand. Drakos gripped it firmly shaking it ferociously in a sideways motion.

'Martanzos bad man,' said Ben 'how you know him?'

'Μεταλλειο βώξίτή' he replied. Having seen it on a map of the area Ben easily recognised that what he said must be at a bauxite quarry.

Apparently Dimos Drakos had a sister who had once lived up in the mountains beyond Varghiani. Souliotes loved mountains, it was their natural habitat. His sister and her husband had been displaced when an open-cast bauxite mine was started near to

157

them by Martanzos. This ended cruelly when, refusing to leave, her husband had somehow lost his life in a mining accident. His sister and he knew Martanzos was responsible.

Dimos had acquired a sort of reasonable English from his days as an engineer on one of the Ben Line ships. He had seen something of the world – at least its ports – but he longed to get home. It was when he returned to this, his part of Greece, that he had gradually become embittered. While listening to him talking about what had happened to his sister - and her husband - Ben sensed an opportunity. If he was that angry, and clearly he was, Ben saw that Drakos might just be able to get his own back a little by giving them a hand as a lookout-cum-bodyguard on the mountain the following day. Leonides would have to talk to him first and assess whether that was a sound idea, and whether he would be willing to join them. They needed someone capable of watching their backs.

Tackling the subject directly, Ben told him the circumstances of their being interested in Parnassos, that a painting from the time of the revolution, associated with the *filiki eteria…* at the mention of the word *philiki*, Dimos leapt out of his seat and, clutching Ben by the shoulder, started a fervent song – not exactly a love song it was more like a dirge, though in a major key. The melody had all the passion and patriotism of an anthem. Thankfully, it didn't last more than a few phrases. Ben was able to catch only a single word, repeated a few times, which sounded like *Zalonga*.

Resorting to the help of a piece of paper, Ben wrote on it the name of the taverna in Tithorea, and the time 10 o'clock clearly by the side of it. He handed it to Dimos, looked at his watch meaningfully and, pointing at '10', adding tomorrow.

Cedric, who had been nursing a beer and only partly listening to Ben, suddenly got up. Pointing towards the road, he said that he had just seen a blue Mercedes with, he felt sure, a recognisable

158

passenger in the back. They must get back quickly.

ooooooo

On their way back Ben told Cedric about the horror of discovering Karamanlis with Martanzos, which meant that he had obviously been lying when questioned by Leonides at the lunch party. What had he to hide?

'It looks as though he must be the source of our leaks.' he said. 'But you don't know him, do you? Karamanlis, I mean. I know his wife tolerably well' He broke off, thinking in fact really quite well, 'though I wonder if she would willingly provide information to her husband about us. Karamanlis and Martanzos are definitely in some sort of business together, I'm sure of it.'

They drove back to Tithorea as quickly as Ben dared, pushing the hire car as fast as it would go. Somewhere ahead of them they would soon see a big blue car. Finally,they drove up the steep narrow road to the village and, in a hiatus of alarm, they saw the same Mercedes coming down the hill towards them. It swished past, with the seat at the back now empty.

Looking at his passenger, Ben realised that Cedric was not enjoying himself one little bit. It couldn't be because he was feeling all at sea, because for Cedric that would have been like a week in paradise. Nor was it because of the way he was driving, at least he hoped it wasn't. No, Ben guessed it must be due to all the comings and goings of the predatory Martanzos. He must be worried about Melina, and naturally he would be looking forward to having some time alone with her. Whatever it was, Ben decided he must leave them to themselves as soon as possible after getting to the taverna.

159

26.

The minute the Mercedes pulled up at the taverna, Melina leapted out and ran amongst the seats under the tree. To her consternation she could see neither of them, no Ben no Cedric. Where could they be? She hadn't realised just quite how badly she needed to see Cedric. Despair began to wrap itself round her like an ill-fitting coat, and at that very moment she became enveloped in a huge hug. Wrapped in Cedric's arms, she began to laugh gently from relief.

'Expecting someone?' he whispered in her ear. Melina gave him a friendly nudge.

'You, you ultra-timid Englishman, why were you hiding from me?'

'Hiding only to seek.... I've been missing you, Melina.'

Ben wondered if this wasn't the moment to leave them, but in an instant Melina was giving him a hug too, with a fondness and warmth that took his breath away. She was back. That was all that mattered. And so, in the nick of time, were they.

'You haven't eaten?' she asked, not grasping that they had also been away.

'No, we haven't. But we are thirsty.' said Ben.

'Why don't we have the Neck of a Horse.' she said with mock pomposity, chiding Cedric by redefining his favourite drink.

Cedric waved for the waiter. Still beaming with joy at being with Melina again, his enthusiasm brimmed over.

'We have been behaving like lunatics.' said Ben 'We didn't follow you but we went as far as Polidrosos, to see a man at a garage - a Souliote by the name of Dimos Drakos. We'll tell you more about him later. How did you get on?'

'You, you really *are* complete idiots' her manner was changing; both men quickly realised from the inflection of her voice that all was not well.

'I don't know where to begin. I need to gather my thoughts. The Horse might help.'

She meant it. Alone in the back of the car, she had believed, but only for a minute, that she might yet find a way out of the whole sorry mess. But she had been too distraught to think straight.

Then, after a sip, she spilled the beans of what had passed between her and Martanzos. In effect he had given her an ultimatum: that he would only guarantee the Englishmen's safety if she would agree to go and live with him. That was the first half, the second was about their safety and it seemed that the need for such a guarantee was real. Martanzos knew very well that their lives were in danger, because he had made the arrangements: he had said to her that a marksman had been hired to shoot them should they decide to venture up the mountain again.

The alternatives were as bald as they were unacceptable: first, she couldn't possibly give in to the grim scheme that Martanzos was proposing – it didn't bear thinking about, not for a second. She would rather die. That she meant it, Ben and Cedric could see all too clearly.

But the other half of the equation, a guarantee of their safety, was every bit as disturbing. No way could she accept the possibility of Cedric or Ben being a target for one of his hired killers. The thought perished. Never.

Which took her full circle. The dilemma was real and it was worsening by the second for she was hemmed in by unacceptable choices. Distraught, her thoughts swirled around in a fog of confusion. What was she to do?

'Actually, there isn't and there won't be a problem.' said Ben 'Don't worry about making choices,' he went on 'you really don't have to. You see, first thing tomorrow,' his voice became marginally louder, recognising the need to appear confident 'at breakfast, Leonides will arrive right here in Tithorea. He brings important news. And,' he went on emphatically 'my new best friend Dimos Drakos will be joining us to provide total, I mean *total* protection from all quarters. He will cocoon us in a safe hoop of steel. We don't have a worry in the world; poor old Zaros Martanzos will have more than he bargained for.'

He was consciously throwing a lifeline to Melina, for he had seen how close to drowning she was.

They stared at him, Cedric in bewilderment, Melina with relief and gratitude. It was clear that the arrival of Leonides changed whatever plans they might be hatching for the following day, bringing relief to both of them.

'I suggest we meet here early tomorrow morning for a - so-called - breakfast, shall we say eight o'clock? Leonides will be here by then. Meanwhile, I must go off and do some long overdue telephoning. I wish you both goodnight.'

He rose, kissed Melina, then muttered quietly to his friend that everything would be just fine in the morning, trust him. He stumbled off into the night. They watched him head off in the direction of the apartment, fumbling for his keys as he walked away.

27.

A very short jog put Ben in the right frame of mind to experiment with another brew of Greek coffee. Using a pack bought from the village shop, whose label showed the sort of strength and flavour that only wet earth can give to a bean, he prayed it would deliver the sort of mudless coffee much preferred by the resident Englishmen.

Throwing a sweater over his shoulders he set off in the direction of the taverna. To his surprise, not only were Cedric and Melina sitting at a table under the oak but, Leonides had also joined them. Leaning forward with an elbow on the table, he was listening to their chatter, puffing away at a cigarette - by no means the first of the day.

'*Καλημέρα!*' said Ben, stretching his Greek vocabulary to its limit. 'Hi, Cedric, these two understood that I've just said Good Morning. But not you. Hadn't you better get a grip and learn to speak the language of the country?'

Unlike Cedric, Leonides beamed with pleasure at Ben's greeting. Apologising for showing up early, he explained that he had used the time well by getting to know Cedric better. Giving a knowing glance towards the couple opposite him, he said he had warned Cedric that he, too, was in love with the Melina, and that in matters of love he was a ruthless competitor. In fact he was overjoyed by what he could see of Melina and Cedric's easy relationship, and happy that they were obviously in love. Cedric asked the waiter for a cup of coffee and a croissant for Ben. All three then gave their attention to the latest arrival from Athens.

'Leonides, you must tell us your news' said Ben.

'Good news, plenty. Nothing but…well... good news. You see.

163

I am giving a lot of thinking to the painting and what it saying. And finally I deciphered the meaning of the white cross. So now we understand painting.' He made a fluttering kind of gesture and finished with a satisfied chuckle.

Well pleased with himself, he beamed confidently at his audience. They, with a mixture of admiration and impatience, were agog. But Leonides wasn't in a hurry to spill the beans. He was savouring the moment like a cat with a dish of cream.

'Go on.' said Cedric, impatient to hear more 'I mean in your own time, of course. You say you have found the key, the actual meaning of …. the white cross, it is a cross isn't it?' still a little sceptical, he was very eager to hear. But Ben quickly intervened.

'Leonides, before I forget. Yesterday Cedric and I met a man called Dimos Drakos from Polidhrosos.'

'The Souliote?'

'Yes. You know him? He absolutely loathes Martanzos. The thing is I've invited him here to meet you as he could be useful. But we'll come back to that.'

Ben leant back in his seat to hear how Leonides had finally uncovered the secret of the painting.

'Yes. No claim it was all my work. No. But I saw connection between white cross and graveyard. Up on plateau beneath the *Mavre Troupe* there is a small chapel, yes?'

'There most certainly is.' It was Cedric, speaking from knowledge gained during their recent exploration.

'And on side of chapel is a graveyard?' This time it was Ben who nodded, for he, too, recollected their visit.

'Very small chapel, *Ayios Georgios* his name, remote, isolated on plateau above Tithorea. Why should have graves'he emphasised the word 'or graveyard?'

He went on to say that the chapel was built for at most a handful of shepherds, with never that many of them living up there at any one time. What he was saying was that few, maybe none, would actually have ended their days there. They would have come on down to their village, to their families. His reasoning turned on accepting that there were never enough shepherds to fill those graves. The numbers involved simply didn't, could never add up. They hadn't died up there. If they thought they might be dying, they would have quickly gone down to Tithorea to be with their relatives. The locals, when called to meet their Maker, were buried where? He paused for effect.

'Here in village, at church I know, named Ayios Ioănnnis Theologos. I think we find, when we look at gravestones on plateau,' he waved his elegant hand upwards ' that the white icon on painting also shows on head of gravestones. White icon, you see, is a cross with white circle looped over top – Greek letter Φ.'

Androustses was sure of his solution; it was totally sound. For, once you accepted that there was a discrepancy between the number of graves and the number of locals in the village, you instantly realised something fishy must be going on.

'Old Androustes, had two kinds of treasure: first gold, but other was antiques – statues and relics from archaeological sites, and statues, icons from churches all over the Peleponnesos. The gold we come back to, but statues, I think we find he buried

165

them, like cadavers in graveyard. How you say? Good place for old bones! It save him moving heavy bodies to Thebes.'

Chuckling with pride, he looked from one to the other of his companions as if challenging them to refute his findings. Ben was first to respond.

'Good God,' he said, 'how beautifully simple.'

Ben instantly saw Leonides's logic. They would obviously need to check the graves around the tiny church to see just what was engraved on the headstones, and then of course what had been buried beneath them. They had a spade, which would come in handy, and they would only need to dig up a few of the marked graves. What an exciting prospect! Ben was itching to start climbing.

But, evidently, not everyone was.

Ben noticed that Cedric had lost most of his earlier enthusiasm; he was no longer responding with anything like the interest he had originally shown. Why had he lost what appeared to be so keen a curiosity, and so suddenly? Sitting next to Melina, he was showing concern at the apparent change in her mood. She seemed deeply troubled. Ben thought he had never seen such a look of anguish on anyone's face. She appeared haunted. What was going on?

A short silence followed, punctuated only by an impatient scuffling of Ben's feet. Consulting his watch, he was aware that the time had slipped by. Preoccupied with such exciting news from Leonides, Ben had overlooked that the friendly mechanic should have put in an appearance by now. If he was coming. It was 10 o'clock.

oooooo

166

'Well we might as well get going' Ben had risen to his feet, looking at his watch as though every second counted. And, struck by the thought that time was costing them something, he said in a voice more suited to a chief executive 'What say we take another look at the plateau? Shouldn't take more than about an hour and a bit to get up there.'

'Yes' said Leonides 'me slow climber. I like admire the view.'

'Admiring the view is always what those who won't give up smoking say. But since you may soon be acclaimed a puzzle solver, you can be forgiven.'

Ben was feeling more and more eager to get climbing, even though he was puzzled by the absence of his new friend, Dimos.

'Cedric will keep you company on the way up, Leonides, but you must keep an eye on him to make sure he doesn't fall over. His element is at sea-level - he's no good on hills. Let's leave in about half an hour from the church. I have a spade, and, Cedric, would you be kind enough to see if you can find some …. er, victuals, I think you call them?'

'Of course.' said Cedric, admiring the new tone of voice being used by his friend, who had morphed seemlessly into expedition leader. Then turning to Leonides Cedric said, 'Doesn't anyone in your country drink ginger ale?'

Cedric had a rather forlorn look about him, fearing problems ahead in sourcing the right victuals, to say nothing of his concern for Melina.

'I mean, my drinking habits are extremely simple, but the want of a decent ginger ale has become serious. Greek brandy doesn't answer with just a splash of soda. The death rattle is no longer muted – it's growing louder by the tinkle of each empty tumbler.'

Leonides showed little concern and, while thinking about it, lit another cigarette. Then from across the space occupied by the taverna's seats and tables there came a dramatic hollering accompanied by arm gestures. Dimos Drakos had shown up.

He rushed over, straight to Leonides and, gripping him by the shoulder, shouted a series of incomprehensible greetings accompanied by a well aimed slap on Leonides's back.

'I have been expecting you.' the tone of Leonides's voice implied that the Souliote was late.
'Good to see you, *athentiko!*' Dimos clearly had a great respect for Leonides, just as he appeared entirely to have forgotten that his new friend, Ben, existed.

'You know each other?' said Ben.

'I'm afraid so.' Leonides wasn't being wholly serious. 'From long ago, Drakos?' he looked fondly at the Souliote 'When the Junta had to be stopped from behaving like Turks. Drakos here appeared from nowhere and started singing songs – mostly about freedom and sex, or were they only about sex?'

'Not sex. Love. Love for country. The song of Zalongas.'

Ben remembered hearing that name. But fearing that if Dimos and Leonides started remembering old times it might interfere with their days climbing, he proposed that Dimos should join them in the climb. Did Leonides approve of that?

'Best idea, Ben,' he said 'but you better know that Souliotes climb like monkeys.'

Dimos hit him quite hard on the middle of the chest, a gesture not lost on Leonides. Drakos then said to him

'No insult Souliote. We climb like angels - not monkeys. We climb?'

'We climb,' said Ben, taken aback by this latest exchange 'we go now.'

28.

Later than planned the party gathered in front of Tithorea's village church. Beyond the railing surrounding the space in front of the church, but by only a few feet, stood the statue of the old warlord himself with his great name, **ΟΔΥΣΣΕΥΣ ΑΝΔΡΟΥΤΣΟΣ**, hewn out of the stone base in bold, rough-cut letters.

Leonides couldn't resist it: welcoming the theatricality of the moment, he stood alongside his ancestor, an infectious grin on his face, virtually taking a bow, perhaps hoping by the magic of osmosis, he might absorb some of the old man's qualities, the better ones. Meanwhile, the sightless eyes of the statue surveyed the plain in silent wonder. Remembering past glories, guessed Ben. To the rest of the party the likeness was striking; there could be no doubting the lineage of the handsome man standing a few feet from the statue.

'Come on Souliotes!' boomed Leonides, 'Let's get climbing or Cedric will die of thirst.'

Ben and Melina led the way, to begin with in the company of Dimos, who was prancing from rock to rock like a goat. The other two, still talking, were shuffling with school-boy reluctance towards the gap in the metal fence that marked the start of the path up the mountain. At first the narrow pathway dropped down about fifty feet from the level of the viewing balcony by means a gully until it reached the face of the slope. The steepness of the drop was a little intimidating, but as soon as they reached the open path on the grassy slope there was sure footing and they took to the foothills of Parnassos like proper hill men. They had a spring in their step.

'Hill men desire their hills!
Who goes to the hills, goes to his mother…'

Ben thought it best not to press on with half remembered Kipling as the rest of the party might think that the thinning air had gone to his head. He increased his stride.

Ben, with his love of walking over hills and mountains, was in a buoyant mood. The air was clean and fresh, the company enjoyable and, importantly, the present quest was a promising one. The chances of discovering buried treasure seemed to have energised them all, making the climb less like hard work.

High up on the first, wide shoulder of the mountain, they gradually approached the outcrops of scrub and rock where, only a day or two ago, Ben and Cedric had had their near encounter with disaster. Ben paused to check the progress being made by the tail-enders, keeping an eye on Cedric's possible reaction when he realised his whereabouts. But they were engaged in a conversation of such profound significance that Cedric failed to pay any attention to where he was, even though he was travelling through the epicentre of his recent nightmare. That's one huge leap forward, Ben Benbow concluded.

He decided that now was as good a moment as any to take to breather, so he and Melina perched together on a rock by the side of the path. Dimos had gone on ahead much earlier with the ease of one who drew added strength from altitude. His brief from Ben and Leonides had been to anticipate any sort of hazard Martanzos might have set in motion on the mountain, specifically that he might have instructed a local hunter to use Ben and Cedric as target practice. Minos had understood precisely just what was wanted and his early disappearance suggested he was taking his responsibilities seriously

The view was truly magnificent. From where they were sitting, a wide panorama spread out in front of them across the endless plain, ending in a smudgy blue haze – the infinity of distance. Their eyes could barely cope with such a vast expanse.

Sitting on the rock, Melina was showing symptoms of pent up nervousness. Ben could sense her unease. Continually turning her head, she was checking to see where Cedric and Leonides had got to, how far they had lagged behind. She was clearly on edge. Ben felt concerned for her, for her general well-being. It occurred to him that she might not feel truly safe up here, high on the steep slope of a mountain. Perhaps, like Cedric, she may have a preference for a flatter sort of earth.

'Melina, I can sense you don't feel entirely happy, sure of yourself. All I can say is that you have no reason to be uneasy - we have a first class line of defence, as it were, in that very fine man, Dimos. You really have no need to be worried.'

For a minute she looked reassured. But he would make a point of staying close to her, for he wanted to be sure that she took in some of the stunning scenery, and enjoyed at least parts of the walk. And she was, Ben thought, worth sticking close to.

Eventually, Cedric and Leonides came up with them. Their vague, shambling way of making progress, walking side by side, had enabled them to discuss a list of edifying subjects including, Ben wouldn't mind betting, one of Cedric's old favourites. He knew that Cedric was interested in the painting materials used by early cave dwellers, a subject that could last for hours. But the distraction and enjoyment of their rambling conversation had helped to take their minds off the physical exertion of climbing. From Cedric's point of view, tramping up a mountain was no light-hearted frolic, especially with a rucksack holding jangling, poorly packed victuals, a picnic that only Cedric could have thought appropriate for the occasion.

Having made sure that all was well with them, Ben and Melina went on ahead again. The gorge forged its way into and up the side of the mountain, from time to time the cut growing deeper. Occasionally, where the edge had fallen away, they caught a glimpse right down to the rocky bottom, the nearly dry river-bed pock-marked erratically with boulders.

To their right, the slope ran upwards until it met the foot of the high limestone wall soaring vertically many hundreds of feet above them towards the sky. At the foot of the escarpment there was a steep run of rocky scree, pieces of loose rock that had fallen from the face of the wall. Highest of all, the summit of Parnassos rose majestically above its surroundings to meet the intense blue of the sky, the peak standing out far above everything else, clear and well defined, like a godly podium set against the sky. The grandeur, the sheer scale of Mount Parnassos also imposed itself on the valley below. And on them. Ben wondered what effect it was having on Dimos. If any.

The path had narrowed and was no more than a few feet wide, sometimes less, and the narrowness of the path made Ben realise that Cedric and Leonides would no longer be able to walk side by side - so with a bit of luck their speed might increase. From time to time the slope grew steeper and the path took to snaking up the incline between the boulders and scrub. The way was mostly clear, but where the vegetation had encroached onto the path they neded to make a detour.

Much to Ben's relief, the climb abruptly came to an end, the path suddenly and unexpectedly opening out onto a lush meadow. To their left stood the old stone water trough for cattle; and, away to their right, hard under the great wall, was a small, white building with a cross on the apex of its roof. They paused, the sight of the small chapel made Ben's pulse race. It wouldn't be long now.

Ben and Melina walked slowly across and up the meadow in the direction of the chapel. They could walk more easily now, with a firm tread on the much flatter surface of the plateau. As they approached, they could see that the roof of the chapel had been retiled in recent times, using tiles that were ordinary, every day tiles. Under the sofit, where the roof overhung the white painted wall, a brass bell had been suspended on a double chain. A short bell-rope was hanging from the clapper. Around the white, stuccoed walls, nature had taken over and the vegetation was growing wild. An oak sapling was quietly growing into a tree.

Ben couldn't see a single gravestone.

ooooooo

No more than twenty to thirty minutes later, Cedric and Leonides emerged from the scrub lining the path onto the wide plateau. As Tom had predicted, having been forced into single file, they had been walking more quickly. Stopping to wave, they continued across the meadow towards the church. From time to time Cedric stooped to pick a flower or inspect a plant or piece of grass that was new to him.

'A fine little chapel.' said Leonides making their final approach. 'I think the graves will be round at the back, under that great wall of rock. Shall we look?'

They skirted along the nearest wall and ducked in behind the far side of the chapel. Overall, it couldn't have been much more than forty feet from end to end. Reaching the far corner, their hearts leapt, for there amid the scrub and another sapling or two, they could just make out the tops of what would certainly turn out to be gravestones. It was difficult to be sure how many there were, for nature had taken over and the undergrowth had spread across everything, covering the gravestones with an unruly tangle of branches.

That the graveyard had been so untended was also encouraging. Where to begin? Ben was the nearest, so he quickly accepted that it should be he who pushed forward through the scrub to take a closer look at the first headstone. He had to clear away the scrub to get there, but even then, because the stone was covered in lichen, he found it difficult to see what, if anything, had been carved on the head of the stone.

'I can't make this out,' he said, scraping it with a twig 'though it looks as though there could be some sort of cross at the top. No, wait a minute.' Using the buckle from his rucksack as a scraper he began seeing more of the engraving on the stone. 'As a matter of fact it may well look like the letter Φ. It just might be a combination of both – a cross, yes, but with the circle of the letter *phi* looped over it. That's it, isn't it, Leonides? As you said – the white cross in the painting has finally delivered its message - with a little help from another Androustes.'

Weeks of puzzling and cleaning, and head scratching had finally come good. George, Ben was thinking to himself, we have a result for you. You were right to trust us.

'Yes,' it was Leonides, speaking in a rather subdued voice 'it was the cross that showed us the way.' He paused, then recovering himself, he said 'I think we need to excavate an actual grave, don't you? I mean let's dig one up. Or do you say dig one down? How about this one? Let's see if we find anything.'

Expectations were mounting. Ben threw aside his rucksack, untied the long handled spade and started hacking at the shrubs. He first started to clear the area immediately around the grave and, when most of the wilderness of weeds and overgrown plants had been cleared, he started to dig. To begin with he struggled to get under the top surface, a layer of coarse grass; eventually, he succeeded in marking out some square patches of grass and cutting through the grass with the blade using his foot on the spade. Then he removed the grass squares by shimmying the blade of the spade underneath and, with a little leverage, he was able to lift each one clear, one after the other. Such clearance takes time, but after an interval he had cleared enough of the grass from the surface. All that remained was soil, a little damp, but now easy enough to dig. He had rather hoped that Dimos would show up and give him a hand. He didn't. So Ben made up an anagram of his name - sod 'im - which made him feel a bit better at having to do all the work.

Before getting on with further digging, and needing some respite from his efforts, Ben – mimicking the old gesture of spitting on his hands – bowed to his audience and intoned an ancient Turkish proverb about luck being in love with the virtuous man. Implying that by doing all the digging he must be virtuous. He got on with his task again, shovelling earth neatly to one side, continuing to heave more and more soil onto the growing heap. When he had dug his way down to about four feet, and the hole was beginning to grow more impressive, he started to flag a little; not surprisingly, for they were up a high mountain and digging deep holes required considerable strength. He enjoyed a brief pause before jumping down into the hole again and continuing to dig and shovel the earth out of the hole.

A few minutes later, he stopped. He had struck something.

oooooo

Not for a minute did any of them expect it to be something like a coffin. Carefully he dug round whatever it was that the spade had struck and soon he bent down to pull at something. Whatever it was didn't move, it was so stuck in the impacted earth. Ben, now quite deep into the hole, stood up and said in a pronounced actor's voice

'Stick in the mud.' He chortled, though no-one else found it

176

that funny, even for what might have been called graveside humour.

But the tension had been broken, and Ben, looking sheepish because of his failed attempt at being funny, redoubled his efforts. Continuing a gentle scraping motion with his shovel, he carefully prized the earth away, little by little, from around the surface of the stone. After a while he bent down again. This time it began slowly to yield to his pulling, and in a short while he lifted out a long thin object bent in the middle.

He passed it to Leonides, and soon after that Cedric handed Leonides his penknife, a much cherished one judging by the initials C.A.S. carved into the wooden casing. Several minutes went by, while the careful removal of earth embedded round the object was slowly chipped away. Leonides, without hurrying, sensitively scraped along its whole length – it must have been somewhere between two to three feet long – until the object slowly revealed itself. It was an unexpectedly shapely arm: starting from the shoulder with gently rounded biceps, it curved round a fine elbow to the fore-arm with its finely detailed veins, finally ending in an exquisitely sculpted hand. A man's arm, that much at least was clear. On closer inspection it looked as though it could have been carved out of Pentelic marble, the grain being close; it also had the sort of luminescence that such a fine quality of marble gives off.

'Well done, Leonides.' said Ben. 'You're a genius. I think a bust of your Androustses head should be placed in the nearest Temple of Worthies. You also deserve a drink, if there is one. But that's Cedric's department. Any idea who this piece of marble might belong to?'

'The form of the arm is rather effete,' commented the restorer, 'suggesting that it is not that of an athlete. And quite young,

I think. Someone's son perhaps. It could come from a torso buried somewhere beneath it, or from a statue in another grave. Beautiful, isn't it?' Cedric was clearly thrilled by the turn of events.

'What I thinking now.' said Leonides. 'Why more digging? No need for digging all of the burial plots, more grave and more grave. We find more of the same, yes? So we dig deeper this plot where there will be more statue. Then each we claim a souvenir before the Antiquities department steps in. Good scheme?'

Ben instantly responded. Speaking with total conviction, he said he wanted no souvenir of any kind, feeling sure that these antiquities, or whatever else they turned out to be, belonged to where they were, here in Greece. They might even belong right here, by which he meant with the people of Tithorea. He paused only to think it through a bit further, then he mentioned the possibility that they could belong to Leonides – a legacy, as it were, from his ancestor.

Leonides declined any claim to ownership, wanting nothing. He offered the explanation that since his ancestor had probably stolen the artefacts in the first place, he would be laying claim to stolen property. But he thought Ben was right, that the locals should have the first claim, but the people to decide this sort of question were from the Department of Antiquities. They would anyway be in charge of the excavation.

Ben grasped precisely what he meant. He only wanted to add that treasure hunting had never been a reason for his coming to Greece. It was really much simpler than that. His real interest had been to solve the riddle of the painting, and he was more than satisfied that they had done just that. The riddle of the relics had been solved, and it was very likely to prove an impressive haul. It had to be up to Leonides to decide what to do as there would be all kinds of formalities.

'Treasure Trove!' warbled Cedric 'Strict procedures must be followed! And by the way, I agree with Ben a hundred percent. We were never in this for plunder; and we're certainly not in the business of stealing antiquities.'

Like Ben, Cedric thought that the proper way forward was for Leonides to decide. It would take time for the experts to unravel the history of the horde, the treasure. Cedric kept repeating the word treasure with enthusiasm. It seemed possible that to celebrate he might break into some sort of hornpipe.

Ben noticed Melina wasn't joining in the celebrating. She wasn't, because she couldn't believe what she had just heard. Something must be wrong. Had she known that Cedric and Ben were really not interested in buried treasure, she could have told Martanzos, there and then, to take a running jump.

And this recent turn of events had unwittingly raised other issues. She realised that Martanzos had never once – and she could remember their conversation word for word – referred to treasure, or treasure hunting, as being the cause of the problem. In fact, he had gone out of his way to say that there was *no* treasure, saying that his branch of the *philiki* had looked into the question and concluded that there wasn't any. No, all that he had said during their lengthy meeting was that Cedric and Ben were 'getting in the way'. He seemed very clear on that score, repeating the accusation many times. In whose way? His obviously, but how could they be in the way?

'Wouldn't it be a rather sweet idea' Cedric was speaking 'if Melina could have some sort of souvenir? I mean being Greek, it would be perfectly in order for her to have something.'

179

'I think she's already got one' replied Ben. 'Unless I'm mistaken, Cedric, you must have given her one of your sovereigns?'

'Perfectly right. I had forgotten. Melina has her souvenir.' He smiled at her with all the warmth and fondness of recollected intimacy. 'Happy with that, my dear Melina?'

'Yes, very!' she said. With that she reached into her pocket and produced a brightened up version of the sovereign Cedric had given her. The gold coin shone brilliantly in the palm of her hand, rays of bright sunlight giving it an added lustre. Even so, she still didn't look the picture of contentment that Ben expected. There was a vacant, far away look in her eyes.

'What I suggest' said Ben, thinking quickly 'is that we take a deeper look into this first hole before we put the arm back where we found it. We can then restore the earth to its original level, and shove the sods of grass back on top.'

Needed no further bidding Ben began digging a little deeper. His spade soon encountered something else, this time a chunky oblong object. In a matter of a few minutes he produced what appeared to be a metal box. Unexpectedly light, he handed it to Cedric. It had markings both on the top and on the sides. Sadly, these were now indecipherable. Cedric managed to open the levered catches and lifted the lid. It was empty. Well, not quite, for there in the corner was a short roll of coins, wrapped in protective paper. Clearly the box must be an old gun-powder tin. At first glance the coins looked like Dutch florins, or even double florins, no more than six or eight of them. Pocketing the coins, Leonides handed the tin back to Cedric. By now Ben had raised himself out of the hole and handed Cedric the spade.

'Everybody seems to be giving me things.' he said in a

grumpy voice. But he bravely jumped into the hole, and began
shovelling back the earth.
In much less time than it had taken to dig the earth out, it was
back. Cedric looking well pleased with himself.

'You may have forgotten' said Cedric, addressing the others in
the manner of a Master of Ceremonies 'but I should soon turn
out to be the focal point of this party. Why? Just wait until…'

He undid his rucksack, and plunging his hands deep inside, he
presented his friends with a bottle.

'Oh, no!' groaned Leonides. 'Not ouzo. Better you ask me. But
we make the most of it. Do you have water?'

'Yes, of course I have. And glasses, though I must confess I
have not been able to source ice.'

He reached further into the rucksack, producing *deus ex machina,*
several stout glasses. In his element as a head waiter, he made
a theatrical fuss over the way he polished the tumblers, using a
scruffy handkerchief. Then, pouring the aniseed distillate into
each glass, followed by adding some water very sparingly, he
made it seem even more precious than the ouzo. Leonides told
him not to be an idiot and, for the love of God, to put much more
water to each glass.

'Yassou!' each toasted their neighbour, followed by a silence as
the taste of the ouzo caught them rather by surprise.

Leonides scanned the slopes above them with a pair of small
binoculars, seeing if he could catch sight of the Souliote. He
couldn't, and folded them away.

Meanwhile Cedric and Melina had gone off for a stroll, out past the overgrown vegetation near the chapel and onto the open meadow. Cedric was thinking what a really lucky fellow he was, how so much happiness was pouring into his life. Chancing to look up, far away at the head of the meadow he caught sight of the gaping hole that was the *Mavre Troupe,* a one-eyed Cyclops staring back blankly in their direction from the face of the wall.

Like many before him, he had been fascinated by the history of the cave, its majestic isolation from the world below. And he wondered about the men and women who had lived there, perhaps as many as forty or fifty at a time, who had dedicated their lives to the long struggle for freedom. Back in those days, life was held cheaply. The cave dwellers – he saw them as moustachioed men in skirts, with several daggers in their belts – must have been every bit as brave as the heroes of mythology. As he swept his eyes across the rocky escarpment he fancied he saw something move near the dark aperture. He couldn't be sure. Having turned away briefly, he looked back for a second time but saw nothing. He must have imagined it.

29.

The would-be gravediggers and archaeologists had been chewing away at the fragments of a meagre lunch, possibly the leftovers from a dish the taverna's cooks had been making for their lunchtime customers. Cedric had bought these few bits and pieces in a desperate hurry, and leftovers was not a word he was familiar with in Greek - but at least it was food. Taking cautious sips from their glasses of Ouzo, the party were disappointed that no wine had come out of his rucksack.

'Now to gold.' Leonides, remembering his promise, sensed this was the moment to return to the subject.

Reaching out his hand towards Melina, he asked to look at her sovereign once again, and went on to say that there was no doubt that the coin was part of the first British loan, the date fitted exactly. At around this time, he went on, old Odysseus was beginning to lose his grip. First, his leadership in the cave had been weakened by a general lack of activity, and second, he was running out of funds. Because so little was happening, there was an air of restlessness among his men in the gloomy cave, often the case when hands are idle. But because he was running out of funds, he was also running out of hope, and despair follows close on the heels of dying hope. His last box of sovereigns was only a quarter full, and he had heard that the arrival of more gold, the second instalment, had gone straight to the newly formed government – where it was supposed to go.

Leonides said that Odysseus's luck had finally run out. So he decided to risk everything on doing one last deal with the Turks, in this case the Pasha of Negropont. Odysseus, having been fighting the Turks since 1823 – five long years – he had also begun to feel physically weary of the long march to freedom. He contacted Ghouras, an old comrade in arms – in fact Ghouras had been his right-hand man in the early years – and packed his bags for Athens. Before leaving, he summoned Trelawney and the others, telling them to bury the booty, both where and how to bury it. Handing to each his share of the dwindling horde of sovereigns, he solemnly bade everyone in the cave goodbye and left for Athens. On arrival the first thing he discovered was that Ghouras had betrayed him. He was promptly murdered, presumably because he wouldn't hand over the cave, or he wouldn't tell his captors where he had hidden the treasure – everyone knew about his treasure.

Leonides thought that Odysseus had had a premonition of the danger that lay ahead even before he got to Athens. And so it was. His end was an ignominious trap: he was strangled and left to hang by a rope round his neck from the Venetian tower on the Acropolis; a grizzly death, but by no means exceptional in this terrifyingly savage revolution.

His followers split up, returning to their old tribal loyalties; war-torn groups that they were, they probably re-grouped somewhere within the government forces.

'By now, nothing was left: no gold and no loyal followers, the second a likely consequence of the first.' Leonides, a good raconteur, had told his tale. 'The purse you found belonged to someone in Trelawney's party. It was the last of the loot, so it was fitting you found it. Well, not quite the last of the bigger pieces of loot as we have just seen.'

The sadness of the tale of the final days of Odysseus and his men had a sombre effect on all of them. Their chatter stopped and silence ensued as each fell to reliving the last hours together of the retinue of partisans: a rousing chorus perhaps, undying oaths of allegiance to each other followed by the melancholy of farewell as they embraced, taking their leave of the cave and each other for the last time. By now, the occupying Turks were being routed,

184

soon to be away on their way for good.

Ben started gathering up the remnants of their picnic, when suddenly, out of the blue, they heard a shot. Loud, a single sharp crack, it echoed off the limestone cliff behind them. They all stopped, frozen in mid sentence, facing each other with troubled expressions.

'What was that? cried Melina, her voice jagged with alarm.

'Someone shooting for his supper' offered Leonides.

'Yes, I thought I saw someone up there – moving about near the cave.' Cedric said, indicating the direction over his shoulder.'

Ben suggested they get themselves ready for the journey back to Tithorea. Getting to his feet, he tied the spade securely to his rucksack, fondly casting a valedictory eye round the ruins of the little village and its chapel. With little sense of regret, he shouldered the rucksack, and turning to the others, repeated his suggestion that they move on down. What would George have made of all this, he wondered? Ben trusted he would have been well satisfied with the result that they had managed to pull off. Sad, though, that he couldn't have been with them.

Turning to the others, he repeated his suggestion that they move on down. But just as they were about to move off across the meadow, there was another shot, much louder this time, probably because whoever was doing the shooting had come much closer, ominously close. They stopped dead in their tracks, a sense of foreboding seeping through each one of them, followed by silence. For there was no doubt that the last shot had been aimed at them. At one of them.

Melina was the first to buckle. Turning to Cedric, she clasped him to her in despair, her face contorted with fear.

'Oh, my God!' she whispered.

'It's nothing,' said Cedric, his hand running down his shin 'just a scratch.'

'What you mean?'

'Here, take a look!'

Cedric was quite calm. He took Melina's fingers and placed them on the back of his shin. There was a tear in his trousers and a little blood. Nothing much, as he had said. If Melina had been frightened she was now horrified. Bending down for a closer inspection she could see that Cedric was right; it was only the barest scratch, possibly from a piece of shrapnel Then she wrapped herself round him almost like a fire blanket.

High above, they could see some sort of movement - possibly the head of a man - bobbing among the shrubs and boulders. The man appeared to be heaving something heavy along the ground, somehow re-arranging things. Soon he stopped, dusted himself down and stood up, waving in their direction.

Leonides let out a guffaw of relief, for hopping down the slope towards them with great élan was the unmistakable figure of Dimos Drakis. He seemed in high spirits. First, he went straight to Cedric and took a careful look at his leg. Satisfied, he moved away and reported to Leonides. Talking rapidly in Greek, using plenty of gestures, he was clearly recounting the facts of the recent shooting episode. Leonides, frequently nodding his head, not only understood, but appeared well pleased with what he had been told. He gave the smiling Drakis a thump on the back - everyone took it to be of congratulation, including Drakos. Reaching into his coat pocket, he pulled out the small roll of Dutch coins; taking one, he flipped it in the air catching it neatly as it came down. Making the gesture of checking to see if was heads or tails, he handed the whole roll to Dimos Drakos. The gift was accompanied by another, friendlier thump.

Having now taken charge of the party, Leonides bid all of them to follow and started across the meadow hotly pursued by the Souliote. Ben walked close to Cedric, who really did seem unharmed. Melina still had his arm.

oooooo

The journey down to Tithorea was uneventful, the walking party thoughtful, not to say hushed. On reaching the start of the village, they gathered in front of the church and Leonides decided that everyone should hear what the Souliote had been up to. He also told Ben that he had already sent a message ahead of them to the police.

Apparently the furtive Dimos had been very active. A mountain scout to his fingertips, he had begun by reconnoitring the whole extent of the mountain they were likely to be on, and a bit beyond for good measure. At the end of his first sweep, he found himself high up, above and well beyond where the meadow ended.

A good vantage point, but to begin with Drakos saw nothing untoward. The first shot gave the game away. A hunter had bagged a deer near where the shoulder turns in towards the gorge right at the top of the meadow. But strangely, he didn't go over to check the carcass of the deer, the first instinctive first step that any hunter would take. The man just left it where it had fallen, and such behaviour had immediately alerted Drakos. He took off, the goat-like mountaineer that he was, shielding himself from view behind boulders and scrub until he had got closer enough to the hunting

187

man. The hunter had found a small plateau and, stretching himself flat on the ground, had propped himself up on a substantial rock. He was studying something through the telescopic sight on his gun.

'Getting ready shooting you or Cedric.' said Leonides. 'Dimos not see who, but guessed one of you. H'e knew exactly what to do.' Leonides spoke tersely, in matter of fact tones.

Picking up a sizeable rock, he noiselessly traversed the short distance separating him from the hunter until he had reached a shrub directly behind the man with the gun. There he held himself ready to act. The hunter was busy adjusting the gun-sight and reloading.

'We hadn't the least idea that a drama was being played out up there above us?' said Ben, chilled by the details of the story so far.

'Thank God, no.' said Leonides through clenched teeth.

A minute or so ticked by. The man with the gun, ready now, began taking careful aim. Fearing that he might be too late, Dimos sprang from behind his hiding place like a tiger and threw his rock at the gunman, hitting him hard on the spine high up the middle of his back. The gun went off, but the man lay still. He had been rendered unconscious.

oooooo

Dimos had clearly meant to kill him, and would have been extremely happy to find he had done so. He had acted impulsively, with no time to think it through. And by the grace of God, he had managed to avert a disaster, in the nick of time. What then followed was Dimos attempting to make it look as though the hunter had fallen on the rock. He felt fairly certain that he had

188

succeeded in this, but the man was heavy. Either way it really didn't matter. He disposed of his own rock far down the mountain.

'Ben, what now we do? We get Martanzos out of his house. Bring him here. Confront him with facts. I know how to do all this…' he broke off with an impatient shrug of his shoulders.

'I noticed you gave Dimos those Dutch coins.' Ben, unnerved, uncertain, wanted to know more.

'Award for brave Souliote. Deserve more, for now is good reward.'

30.

Stephanos Driakis, the second most senior figure in the local police force, soon put in an appearance. Parking his car some distance from the church, he came straight over to Leonides and the others. He looked flustered.

'There is a problem?' he enquired, knowing perfectly well what had happened.

After the telephone call from Leonides, the mountain rescue services had ordered a helicopter search of the upper slope for the wounded hunter. First, a dead deer was spotted, confirming that a hunter had been at work. And not long after that they saw what was obviously the body of a man. Having located him, they picked him off the mountain and flew him to the hospital at Livadia. He had regained consciousness, but was suffering some sort of back injury from a fall.

'Yes, Driakis' came a curt reply from the increasingly commanding presence of Leonides 'there *has* been a major problem. But you will also know this already. A man had an accident high up on the plateau, requiring medical assistance, possibly intensive care.' He was looking at the policeman squarely, dark eyes penetrating to the core of his being. 'But there is another complication.'

'What do you mean?' said Driakis, abruptly jerking his head round towards Leonides. His interest had become razor keen.

'Near the church up there, the chapel of Ayios Georgios, we found what we were looking for – a large quantity of antiquities.' Watching the policeman as he spoke, he was not disappointed. His eyes had narrowed and a look of terror began spreading across his face. 'Yes, Driakis, many, many antiquities. You must include that in your report. And make sure that the Department of Antiquities in Delphi has been alerted, won't you? I have spoken to the Minister in Athens already.'

There was no doubting who was in charge, of the interview at least. If Leonides had asked the policeman to stand to attention he would probably have clicked his heels together.

'You know what this means, don't you? That whole area up there has become a Site of Special Archaeological Interest, an officially designated site, an SSAI. That makes it subject to an immediate quarantine – no trespass of any kind anywhere on the land, no shepherds, no sheep, no hunting, no walking, nothing; the area has got to be completely cordoned off. By your department I should think. It will remain so until the Department, having done its work – and there is much to do – gives the all clear. That will be in about five years time, at the their rate of work.'

Leonides was pleased with how his outline of the changed state of affairs had gone. Having telephoned the Antiquities Minister, whom he knew, and told him what had been found, the Minister in turn had told him what procedures would have to be followed. But what really interested Leonides now was the reaction of the policeman. He was dumbstruck, as though his world was about to collapse. His first reaction was to get in touch with headquarters, they would have to know what had happened. He also knew that there was an even more awkward task ahead; someone, not him he hoped, was going to have to contact Mr Martanzos. Driakis could see the storm clouds gathering, huge billows of trouble, and he didn't fancy his prospects of survival.

Excusing himself, he walked back to his car and got on the radio. The upshot was worse than he had feared – and to cap everything he had been told it was his job to contact Martanzos. What bothered him now was less the confrontation with Martanzos, difficult though that was going to be: no, it was the ensuing hiatus that looked bad for him. Would he be able to hang on to his pension, was the question uppermost in his mind. After thirty years of slogging it out in uniform he wondered if he might soon have to open a business repairing shoes. It was that bad. He walked over to the small metal telephone kiosk and took a deep breath.

Martanzos went off like an incendiary rocket. When he came back to earth, there could well have been ice on his upper lip he was so angry. The only good news for Driakis was that his chief, an obsequious official with connections at every level of the regions community, was clearly marked out for most of the blame. Driakis didn't fancy being in his boss's shoes. But it looked as if his own pension might still be safe. Zaros Martanzos had told him to wait near the church until he arrived.

Ben could also see the policeman's face, as he sat in his car talking on the radio telephone. Things were obviously not going well for him. Ben had been following the interview – as choreographed by Leonides – going almost to the letter. He watched the final few seconds of their encounter as expressions of growing anxiety crossed the poor man's face.

'We have about forty minutes' said Ben 'and then, exactly as you predicted, our man Martanzos will be here. Do we need to involve Cedric? In some respects it might be better if we kept him and his condition under wraps.'

'Exactly so, Ben. Will you see Melina Ok too. What she say will be a hammer blow. She must be in the frame of mind, feeling OK.'

'Will do. She'll be fine. I'll be back when they are both sorted out.'

Ben left Leonides chatting with Dimos Drakos, perhaps reliving past escapades, wallowing in the memory of some no doubt very dubious activity. He noticed they were standing a safe distance apart. Thank God for that, Ben thought as he walked away.

oooooo

Ben found Cedric and Melina at a table of the taverna and joined them. Coming to the point, he told them that Martanzos would be arriving at the church in half an hour. They had to get themselves ready. He explained to Cedric that it might be better if he didn't put in an appearance, at least not to begin with: he could watch from a secure spot, perhaps in the church or nearby, where he couldn't be seen. It was vital that Cedric kept himself hidden as they might want to frighten Martanzos into thinking that he had been badly hurt, possibly fatally. Was that OK by him?

'Of course, Ben, whatever suits.'

Ben explained to Melina, that she was needed as a key witness. She must make sure she was ready to stand her ground when confronted by Martanzos.

'Will you be up to it?'

'You'd be surprised.' she said, turning her head away slightly.

Ben, realising that Melina may not have had time to recover from the trauma of the shooting, sensed the need to bolster her confidence. Warm food had to be part of the answer, a bulwark against the onslaught of Martanzos.

'Grand. Let's grab a quick bite to eat, here.'

Melina said she would have the same as they were having and excused herself briefly to fetch a sweater. Ben ordered some light food and two more beers. Cedric was looking rather out of sorts. Too many unpleasant things had happened to him recently, making him wonder how much more he could take - even someone hard of hearing could tell that his death rattle had become ferociously noisy.

31.

Sitting inside the chapel, Leonides explained to Ben and Melina what he planned to do. Certain that the Regional Police, including Stephanos Driakis, were under the influence of Martanzos, his idea was to draw Martanzos out of his lair. So far, so good; he appeared to have swallowed the bait. When he gets here, Leonides said he intended to confront him with the facts: that the shooting had been carried out on his orders, as had the earlier attempt on Cedric's life and the murder of his cousin, George. If necessary, Melina could be brought in to corroborate parts of this.

Leonides thought Martanzos's guilt would be undeniable, though he would certainly bluster and become volatile; his connection to these events would be self-evident. The only aspect of the whole affair that still troubled him was trying to fathom his motive for the eradication of anyone who strayed across his path on Parnassos. Melina had said that Mantanzos repeatedly mentioned that the two Englishmen were *getting in the way*. In whose way? His, clearly, but why?

'Antiquities are of no interest to a man like him. H'e too busy mining. But, but wait a minute: if his interest was mining, his problem with people 'getting in the way' must be getting in the way of mining'. Then it come to me. Martanzos must want the mountain above Tithorea for mining. You see, in region north-west of the Parnassos is plenty bauxite.'

'Of course.' Ben only wished he had read something useful at university, like geology, as he might have put two and two together much sooner. 'So what you've done is send him a message that mining is not possible in this area?'

'Yes. The policeman has spoken him direct, or through his boss, saying antiquities are found near the chapel, that the

195

whole area cordoned off and now have special status. Nothing be done or touched. The whole area in limbo. And, knowing how slow Department of Antiquities move, limbo last long.'

They talked on for some time, Melina taking both of them through the details of her interview with Zaros Mantanzos. Having been given to understand that nothing would happen before tomorrow evening at the very earliest, she had been taken by surprise by today's events. But, like everything else Martanzos had ever said or done, he had not kept his side of the bargain.

The pieces were beginning to fit together now, except for one thing. Ben noticed that Melina's face, normally tanned and lively, had gone as grey as a rain cloud, drained of all colour. Her eyes, too, had taken on a distant, faraway look. Difficult to put into words, but the change in her complexion made Ben uneasy.

Just then a car drew up outside the church. In the growing dusk it looked blue, quite new and very probably German.

oooooo

Leonides leapt to his feet and shot out through the church doors, leaving Ben and Melina sitting side by side in the church. Close to the rererdos in a shadow Ben could make out the outline of a figure, none other than Dimos Drakis.

Outside it was eerily quiet. Having dropped its passenger, the blue Mercedes slid silently away and parked in the street leading from the church, facing down the hill, ready for its return journey. Coming from opposite directions the two men met, face to face, in the area immediately in front of the church; the curved arena and the dying light providing a strikingly theatrical setting.

'So you respond to my summons.' Leonides's deep voice

196

was authoritative; speaking in Greek, he glared at Zaros Martanzos.

'What is going on, what are *you* doing here?'

'You should have no need to ask. A short while ago, Cedric Simmonds, a young Englishman, was shot – perhaps fatally -, miles up there on the plateau.' He pointed with his arm up the face of Parnassos. 'He was standing next to me at the time. But I was in no danger. The single shot that nearly killed him was well aimed – clean, almost lethal – so well aimed that it could only have been the work of a marksman.'

Leonides paused, head tilted back a fraction, every line and angle of his body a threat to his adversary.

'In effect, it was attempted murder.' he said at last. 'He was my guest – my *proxthenos*. You, Martanzos, even you will know will know the meaning of *proxthenos*.' Leonides spoke his words with animal menace 'You will know its exact meaning.'

Pausing, he let his message sink in, and it was clear from the look on Martanzos's face that it had. He began to look like a man searching for the exit.

'I know' continued Leonides 'you're not interested in statues and stuff like that.'

'Of course not.' said Martanzos 'Torsos, armless athletes, all that leaves me cold. I am a miner. That's my interest. I like digging wealth out of the soil, out of the earth we stand on - and particularly out of mountains.'

'You are talking about bauxite? Well, you now have another problem. Earlier today a large quantity of antiquities –

statues, artefacts, church icons and much else besides – was discovered on the plateau above Tithorea. Such a find will have to be excavated properly, and painstakingly, by the relevant specialists in order to decide how the State should proceed.'

'You can't be serious. You're making it up!' Mantanzos spat out the words, like unwanted olive stones. 'My Company has been granted Mineral Rights by the Regional Government, granted with enthusiasm I should add, to mine the whole area of the plateau to the right of the Gorge, and the shoulder beyond it. These slopes of the mountain are rich in mineral reserves – mostly bauxite. Record ore levels, levels of more than 70% aluminium ore, have been found over the whole area. Mining on this scale will bring great wealth to the region, greatly benefiting the regional economy.'

'The Department of Antiquities will of course be the arbiter of any dispute over the right to mine, but I wouldn't hold your breath. The decision to close the area off has been taken already, in fact the whole plateau has been declared a Site of Special Archaeological Interest. You don't stand a chance.'

Leonides spoke with complete assurance and, as he did so, he stepped forward, closer, placing himself within easy reach of the smaller man.

'But it is not antiquities I want to talk to you about. I want to talk to you about having people killed. Murder.'

Emphasising the last word, Leonides saw Martanzos take an involuntary step back from their confrontation.

'You see, the man killed on the ferry from England to Holland, George Abbott - his real name was Georgios Androustes - was my family, a cousin. It was you who ordered his murder.

198

And that, Martanzos, makes you his murderer.' Leonides was glowering at him with raw antagonism. 'Next, an attempt was made a few days ago on the life of Cedric Simmonds. One of your men tried to push him into the Velitza Gorge. He escaped, but only very narrowly.. This too, an attempted murder, was also on your orders.'

Martanzos, struggling to contain himself, had both his hands in the air, as if poised to reach Leonides and grab him by the throat.

'Then, today. Another attempt was made on the life of the same Englishman, Cedric Simmonds. He was shot by someone using a high velocity rifle, very probably an AK 57. You may not have pulled the trigger, Martanzos, but the marksman was acting on your orders. You ordered his killing. And,' pausing to add weight to his words 'had he succeeded, that act would again have made you a murderer. A double murderer,'

At that precise moment Martanzos noticed through the open door of the church two figures seated inside. He noticed Ben, whom he didn't recognise; and then he saw Melina. Who? How could she be in the church? And in that fraction of a second he understood that the whole facade of his life was crumbling, about to fracture in pieces around him. Forced to see the truth, the ultimate showdown that all who have trussed themselves up in a web of lies and deceit must eventually face, he shook his head. He saw that a single thread of truth can, on its own, unscramble an entire edifice of deceit. In this instance, of course, it was Melina: she knew the truth. Seeing her, stopped him in his tracks. Sitting next to a man, possibly an Englishman, she couldn't have been more thirty feet from where he stood. His brain raced.

oooooo

Inside the chapel, Ben was looking enquiringly into Melina's

199

dark eyes. She was disturbingly beautiful. But it was her eyes that cautioned him, they seemed to have undergone a sea change, to have become focussed on the infinity of distance. Her eyes seemed to have become fixed, not with remorse, no. It was revenge. They had become fixed on revenge. He was quite taken aback. Shaken.

Between them dumped on the mosaic floor stood her hand bag. It was a voluminous one for keeping things of little consequence in, a sort of portable attic. In dropping it on the floor, the handles had fallen apart, opening it at the top, revealing to Ben's curious gaze much of its immediate contents. From being taken aback, he now became horrified. For, if he was not mistaken, what he was looking at was the butt, the handle of a revolver. No doubt about it. It was certainly the grip of some sort of pistol, not a very big one, but definitely a hand-gun. This discovery, added to the strange look in Melina's eyes immediately rang loud alarm bells. Her reason for having a pistol in her bag may not have been immediately obvious. But Ben, exceptionally quick witted in such circumstances, knew exactly why. He must act, and quickly.

Looking up at the ceiling of the church for inspiration, he saw a painting of the infant Christ in the arms of his mother. No inspiration there, but wait, perhaps it would do. It would have to do. Pointing at the icon, he asked if she could explain the difference between the Orthodox version of the Madonna and the one revered by the western or catholic church. Following his train of thought she rose saying there was no real difference she was aware of, and as she was speaking she looked up at the icon to make sure she hadn't missed anything obvious. In that fleeting second, Ben reached into her bag and, snapping his fingers round the small weapon, removed it to the safety of his pocket. He had done it. Undetected. Phew! Melina, seeing Ben's interest shift to the church door, followed his gaze. It had swung a little further open so they could now see the two men facing each other outside. Ben was unmoved by what he saw outside; but when Melina looked she was horror struck. Martanzos was staring at her.

She reached for her bag and looped it over her shoulder. Rather too nonchalantly, thought Ben. Both then moved towards the door, as if drawn by a powerful magnet, Melina first, but closely followed by Ben. Very closely.

Outside there was still a residual line of light low in the western sky. The street lamps round the the area had been turned on, shining on the adversaries as they stood poised in virtual combat in a pool of light. Standing there, locked in a fierce exchange of words,their expressions were easily discernible. There was a raw, terrifying antipathy between them. Hearing footsteps coming towards them, Leonides turned as Melina made her way out of the church. The moment was charged with danger. Ben was keeping close to Melina, alert for anything she might attempt to do. Very, very close to her.

'I believe you know each other?' Leonides, looking straight at Melina, made a gesture of introduction towards Martanzos.

'We do.' was all she said, probably all she was capable of saying.

32.

The two men standing in front of the church had been attracting the attention of several villagers on their way home. The locals were soon loitering around the wrought-iron fence in small clusters of two or three people. Mostly quite elderly folk, they were showing a keen interest in the match being played out between the two antagonists. It seemed to them that a contest of high drama was being played out, a situation likely to get even more dramatic as the evening wore on. Their attention had been drawn to it in the first place because the men's voices had been growing louder and louder during their confrontation. Now, something more sinister in their body language encouraged the spectators to think that a last, dramatic twist was about to unfold. The locking of horns had taken on a more gladiatorial significance: there was an edge to it, a potential excitement well beyond the norm of village gossip. This was gripping stuff.

Not only were the two men oblivious of the growing audience, both had also failed to notice that a clearing through the swelling crowd had also developed. As if by some unseen natural force, a gap had formed and in it there now stood a woman. She was elderly, and wore a black cotton scarf over her head, tied under her chin – the fashion long decreed for widows of the parish. She had been listening to every word the men had been saying. The need to hear more was over. She walked away to her front door, knowing that the time had come to act, and within a short while she had returned to the gap.

That was the moment when Ben and Melina made their unexpected appearance. Zaros Martanzos, slowly beginning to lose his grip, was now more or less pinned to the spot he had stood on from the start of the confrontation. He was jabbering away about something that made little sense either to Ben or Leonides, waving an outstretched arm in the direction of Melina.

Melina stepped forward as calmly, as if she might have been walking into a shop, ferreting around in her bag as she walked. Looking intently in the direction of her tormentor, her voice choked with pent up emotion, she said that as God was her witness, Zaros deserved to die, and that she would willingly sacrifice her own life to make sure he paid the price for his crimes - the murder of her mother - and the attempted murder of the man she loved. He was a double murderer. But her step was slowing as she walked forward, faltering until she had reached a standstill. Her hand had ceased its feverish searching.

It was then that the widow in the gap of the crowd started to move: head up and shoulders back, she surged forward in the direction of Martanzos. With her first few steps she seemed to imitate a sprinter, for she crossed the short space in front of the church at speed, reaching the point where Leonides and Mantanzos were standing. Before anyone had noticed her. Ahead of Melina, she now stood in the space between the two men. They had moved slightly apart as Melina approached.

But the widow was not to be distracted. She knew exactly what she must do and how to accomplish her mission. Going straight up to Zaros Mantanzos and, standing directly in front of him, she pulled from the folds of the black shawl wrapped round her shoulders a long kitchen knife and plunged it deep into his chest. Unobstructed by anything like a rib bone, the blade penetrated his heart. He dropped to the ground clutching at the knife handle, already too weak to draw it out. The widow stood back. Then, falling to her knees, she crossed herself muttering an inaudible prayer as an epilogue, her lips moving silently. Her work was done, the death of her husband had been avenged. A gasp of horror went up from the small crowd of onlookers. The tragedy had played itself out. It was over. Nearly.

From behind the small group of participants in the drama, a small, wiry man with flaring moustachios strode out to the widow, lifted her up and took her gently by the arm. Together, he and his sister walked slowly away through the silent crowd; and as they walked, arm in arm, they were singing their own timeless song, the proud song of their ancient homeland. Ben had heard it once before.

It was the song of the Zalongas.

33.

Ben Benbow, alone in Leonides's drawing room, was waiting for a phone call to confirm his flight back to London. On the table in front of him were a few items belonging to Cedric, prominent among them was his penknife and passport. The knife, as Ben had seen up the mountain, had his initials carved into the wooden barrel of the casing, C.A.S. Cedric had said it was a treasured talisman, inherited from his mother's side of the family.

Fascinated to learn what the 'A' stood for, Tom turned to the last page of Cedric's passport and saw that 'A' stood for d'Arcy. This revelation made Ben scratch his head for there was something familiar about that name. He trawled through his memory recalling details of the many excerpts he had read during his stay in Greece. And, yes, he had it. The last time he had come across it was in an extract from the paper he had been given by the British School in Athens. It related to the arrival at the cave above Tithorea of a certain Major d'Arcy Bacon, late of the 19th Light Dragoons. That was in 1826.

The energetic major had come to the rescue of Edward Trelawny, immobilised in the cave by a bullet received during an attempt on his life by a young British army officer. The Major had somehow managed to engineer Trelawny's passage out of Greece on board an English frigate. An eccentric figure, he had been on an extended walking tour of Russia, the Balkans and other neighbouring countries of the Ottoman Empire. Before turning for home, he decided to see what life was like in revolution-torn Greece. It was thought, perhaps uncharitably, that his prolonged absence from home might also have been provoked by the need to escape from his creditors, notably his elder brother.

Was he an ancestor of Cedric's? It would be too wonderful if that proved to be the case. There would be something rather fitting that a descendent of the earlier d'Arcy should have come to Greece and, once again, rescued someone in distress; not a Cornishman this time. He had rescued a woman with corn coloured hair and an alluring voice.

Both of them were coming round for a cup of tea in less an hour. Ben's bags were packed, and if he was lucky enough to get the phone call, he would be catching the last flight to London. Leonides was going to drive him to the airport.

If all life is an experience, then being driven to the airport by Leonides could turn out to be an experience too far. But assuming nothing fatal happened on the way, the journey would at least bring home to Ben the joy of still being alive. And being alive reminded him that, within a matter of only a few hours, he would be back in London and with Gill, and there was nothing in the world that he would rather look forward to than the prospect of seeing her.

There they were! He heard Lela giving Melina a welcoming kiss in the hall and, seconds later, she was hugging Ben, as though his clothes would fit better after the intimacy of such a pressing. When he had disentangled himself, he took Melina over to the table where he had been sitting. She told him that Cedric had been ambushed by Leonides and would follow shortly.

'I've just discovered that Cedric had a middle name.' he said. 'Apparently it was d'Arcy. Does that ring a bell?'

'No, should it?' The voice replied, oblivious of its effect.

With a look of bemused surprise, she was shaking her head and her lovely corn-coloured hair was floating gently about her face.. Having recovered much of her lost self-assurance, her energy levels were dangerously high.

'Not at all. May be it's just a coincidence. I'll check it out when I'm in London. By the way, I hope your coin is safe.'

' You bet.' she said.

'Please make sure these all get back to Cedric, he's rather careless with his belongings.'

For a brief second it seemed as if she might have been on the point of asking him about something else. As no mention had ever been made about its disappearance, Ben knew she must have been puzzled by the disappearance of her small hand-gun and she might have suspected him. Having given it to Leonides, as far as he was concerned the subject was closed. But Melina did have something she wanted to say.

'You know, the little ceremony up on the mountain by the chapel was something I'll cherish till the day I die. A magical light was playing on the plateau that afternoon, creating an arc of wonderful colour on the high shoulder behind us.' She spoke with great tenderness. 'That was a touching little ceremony Leonides concocted, wasn't it?

Her expression briefly took on a distant dreaminess.

'The little headstone was beautiful, wasn't it? The clever old fellow must have pulled a few strings to get that done so quickly. And he must have pulled quite a few more to allow us to go up there at all, close to so much treasure. I thought the carved stone cross looped with a Φ, with all our names carved on it was a lovely touch. He was right to create a permanent reminder of our quest in search of his family's treasure.' She paused. 'Did you realise that the wind blowing through the grove of trees was the oracle whispering cryptic messages?'

'I heard it.' said Ben. 'These days I seem to spend a lot of time listening to far off melodies, which makes me think I should get back to London. It also sets me off wondering about that other song, the song of the Zalongas. You said when we had recovered ourselves you would tell me where it came from. That sad old melody haunts me, mostly when I'm barely half awake; I should love to know where it comes from and how it comes to be so beautiful.'

'The song of the Zalongas does have a sort of ghostly charm about it; it's.... it's so melancholy.' Melina spoke softly. 'But first let me tell you about Parnassos. The melodies we heard were the choral voices of the muses, sighing for the happiness as well as for the sadness of the human condition.' she stopped, sighing briefly, before finishing ' Taken all together they talk of love.'

Ben recalled Yeats's lovely lines

'Plato there and Minos pass,
There stately Pythagoras,
And all the choirs of love.

Buoyed up by the poem, he wanted to wish Melina all the good fortune in the world and hoped she would hear the choirs of love for ever. But all he could manage was a smile, a smile of shyness.

'Now the dance, the song of the Zalongas,' Melina continued, 'that is very different music. Special to the Souliotes, dating from the beginning of time when they roamed free among the mountains of Albania. In reality it is a song of defiance.'

Ben wanted to know more, more about their sure-footed dancing, as well as the origins of their national song. Yes, Melina said

208

she knew all about that. Apparently the Souliotes were ferocious fighters, hardly ever losing a battle even after so many attempts to subdue them. But in the end the Ottoman Turks overwhelmed them. The final encounter was in 1803, which ended when twenty-two Souliote women were trapped by the Turks in a ruined castle. Rather than surrender to the soldiers of the Turkish army, they committed suicide. The gallant twenty-two jumped off the high cliff of the castle into oblivion, and as they went to their death they danced and sang - they sang the very song that Dimos Drakis and his sister sung that night, the Song of the Zalongas. Tom was greatly moved by this little epic, because he was remembering Dimos and his sister calmly walking off into the black of night singing away with childlike confidence in the words and meaning of their heart-rending song.

The next thing he knew was that Leonides, followed closely by Alex and Cedric had come into the room. Having casually pushed the door open they both stopped for a second while Melina finished her story. But they had a pressing need to see Ben because a call had come and time was short. Leonides had a very small bundle under his arm. Making an effort, he coughed noisily and propelled himself towards the centre of the room.

'Please, excuse.'

He stopped, uncertain how to continue in the emotionally charged circumstances. But he needed to make a presentation, and time was getting seriously short. With an assumed formality he cleared his throat and spoke in a steady voice

'Alex and I , and Cedric and Melina, would like to present you with a small souvenir.' He offered up the badly wrapped bundle, which had been under his arm, putting it on the table in front of Ben with a flourish of formality. 'And by the way, the airport rang to confirm you were on the flight.'

209

'Whatever is it?' said Ben. 'Not a painting?' he smiled mischievously.

'Not on your life, Ben.' said Cedric, 'Besides, your restorer looks like being busy for the foreseeable future.'

Ben started to unwind the poorly wrapped parcel, which wasn't difficult, for the cloth wrapping had already fallen away. It was the size of Ben's hand.

It turned out to be the letter Φ carved in dark wood of unknown origin. Small, with a fine patina, it had an unmistakably antique provenance.